Axing My Exes

Jerrica Zeron

This book is dedicated to every girl who has ever had an ex she just can't seem to get rid of.

To Rick and Joyce. Without your superb baby-making skills, I wouldn't be here. Your constant support and faith in all of your kids is inspiring. Sorry for all the cussing and mentions of boobs.

Jerrica Zeron

Chapter One

A Girl Has Gotta Eat

More than a bottle of wine in, Scarlett and I start the inevitable cliché tipsy-girl discussion: the men we've had sex with.

My best friend starts. "Okay, so there was Leo, Alejandro, the orthodox Christian, the magician, the guy from Kentucky, New Zealand...Mmmm, New Zealand knew exactly how to please a woman with his—"

I raise my hand in the air stopping her from going on. Yuk yuk yuk. Squeezing my eyes shut is not helping to erase the images starting to form in my head. Damn my overactive imagination. As I open them, I see a naughty smile stretched across Scar's face. I definitely do not want to know what she is thinking about. "Please tell me you did not have sex with a whole country, and that you can at least remember the first names of the men you've let penetrate you."

We start laughing. Finding my quip funnier than she does, I laugh harder. Standard. Or maybe I'm just a lightweight.

When the wine kisses the inside of my cheeks, I can't help but smile and giggle with pure childlike joy. Merlot and I have a very solid relationship-I give it housing and it gives me happiness.

Scarlett pauses for a second to get her thoughts in order, which is looking more like head banging than focusing.

She slams her hands down on the sofa. "Alexandria, if we're going to start throwing out names, you better get a pen and paper. I want to remember this in the morning!"

A quick traipse to the kitchen finds me rummaging in the random-crap drawer for a pen and paper. My goofy skip to the living room lands my petite body back on the couch. If I didn't weigh less than one of Santa's elves, that plop could've seriously damaged the springs holding the fluffy cushions together. The red-inked pen hits the paper with purpose as I start giving names to these human beings.

Scarlett finishes her list of, surprisingly, only eight men, bringing us to the conclusion that she needed to start sleeping around. I mean, we are in our prime. It's a fact that our twenties will only last a decade, so she should hop on a few more pops to flaunt the fact that her boobs are still closer to her chin than her stomach.

I finish my list and squint at the page. I was only two men sluttier than Scar? Yep. That's my number, and I'm sticking to it. I don't have to count one-night stands or vacation flings, right? Just the ones I actually had feelings for.

Ugh, feelings. I wish they didn't exist in our genetic make-up. Everything would be so much easier if that was the case. I remember thinking that dehydration was imminent after all the crying when Number 4 left, or more accurately, *I* left, because he never showed up. Splash in some humiliation and rejection, then tada! I became really good at shutting my emotions off. An expert at it, in fact.

Ouch! I grab my chest. What's that? Why is my heart hurting? I look down at the list again. Shit. These idiots must still occupy a spot in that red-thumping-thing in my body. And seeing their names is making it beat quicker, but also making me think of how hot they all were. What a bunch of studs! The ass on Number 3, mmm mmm! Well, now it's impossible to focus on my increasing heart rate because the thought of those hunky bods is sending a welcomed tingle to my lady-parts.

I proudly announce, "Hey, Scar. All of these dudes are super sexy in their own way, aren't they?"

"Yes, good for you, you slut," she grumbles while laughing into her wine glass. "Attractive, successful men just fall for you. You are tiny and fit with big boobs and big blue eyes. You walk into a room and three different men are thinking to themselves, *I want to put a baby in that woman.* It is extremely annoying, actually."

I throw my head back at that ridiculous comment. She was obviously joking. Men didn't really do that, did they? And here I thought impregnation was the last thing on the modern man's mind. Crazier things do happen, I suppose. Though, I kind of like the idea of me having an attraction super power. *You there in the blue jacket and blond coif, you will fall in love with me now.* Ah, if only. "That would be a neat trick if it were true, but these hips do not scream *holder of your future child.*" I accidentally snort. "If anything, they say *I belong on an adolescent male.*"

I continue snorting as I chuckle into my wine glass before taking a classy large gulp. "It is true that I have been lucky with men. It may be because I am kinda like a dude, so these guys are just like, *hey, here is a hot chick with a brain that I can hang with and stick my dick in, I think I will keep her around for a while.* There is no secret or scam."

My fluffy white Persian cat, Vera, sneaks onto the couch, wanting to join the party. Scarlett picks her up, moves her beside her face and talks in a baby voice to the blue-eyed feline princess. "Well, we now know for sure that narcissism is not a characteristic your mommy is lacking. If her ego gets any bigger, there may not be any more room in here for you."

Frowning at Scar, I grab Vera and pull her onto my lap. How dare she try and turn my cat against me? Vera's not a puppet. She's the best cat on the planet, and I'm not just saying that because she's mine. Okay, maybe I am.

Vera starts fussing around so I pick her up and let her outside onto our oversized balcony. She loves to be out, watching all of the commotion on the busy street below. Ah, to have the life of a feline; eat, sleep, and people watch. How perfect would that be!

When I return to the living room, I see Scarlett sticking her tongue down to the bottom of the wine glass, refusing to miss the last drip. How she reaches to the end of that large balloon-like shape, I don't know, but I like where her head is at—don't waste what the Good Lord, and the vineyards of Chateau Trotanoy, gave us.

My mind returns to the five-minutes-ago conversation. "Okay, so maybe my ego is a little inflated. But I don't see anything wrong with being confident. Men are attracted to that quality, you know." I tilt my head back as I also finish my glass. "But you're exactly the same, so we're in this narcissistic bubble together."

My eyes water since that gulp went down the wrong tube. Coughing seems like the cure, but it's making it worse.

Scarlett leans closer and gives me a few whacks on the back. Okay, so maybe I could have taken the rest in two separate sips. But I can't be falling behind. A true friend never makes you think you're drinking too fast. That would be rude. Scar is like my sister from another mister, so this probably won't be the last time I nearly choke on Merlot for her.

She laughs at my struggle. "The speed you reel them in would suggest we're not even in the same ballpark, honey."

Ugh. I hated being called *honey*. Something in Scar's tone prompts me to take a longer look at her. Could she be resentful of something I had no control over? I didn't wear a neon-sign asking men to flock to me. Couldn't all these years of friendship sustain the latent animosity I perceived?

Scarlett and I have been best friends for twenty one years. We spent twelve of those years growing up traveling the world because of our fathers' professions, and living through the hell of being home-schooled on the road. The upside was the thousands of adventures we went on and the foreign ass we met along the way. We roomed together in university in the UK, lived with our respective boyfriends for a few years in different countries, then moved back in with each other in downtown San Francisco when we realized our friendship is better than any relationship we've been in. Toxic, we know. Following that revelation, we got illegitimately married while on the back of a camel on vacation in Morocco. A promise of our everlasting friendship and love is what we tell people. And by people, I mean my mother.

Ah, to think of that crazy lady who willingly gave birth to four children naturally, without any help from medication, at all. Nothing. Four kids. Who does she think she is?

Superwoman? Well, I guess she kind of is. I did grow up in the best, craziest, most entertaining and smotheringly loving family you could ever imagine. Let's just say that if my mother were okay with sharing my dad's spare time with a camera crew, we would be bigger than any half-witted reality TV family.

You have no clue who my dad is, right? Let me enlighten you. My father is Frederick Green, loving father of four, loyal husband of thirty-five years, and *the* famous Formula One driver. Scarlett's father was an F1 driver, too. Growing up with racecar-driving dads meant traveling a lot. This usually fucks up kids completely, but for us, it didn't. Well, we aren't perfect but it's not like we torture kittens or anything.

Scarlett's parents divorced when she was three. When they sat her down and told her the news, her response was *I think that is for the best*. She had already developed an adult-like independence. She also had an adolescent *I'll do whatever I please* attitude, which I call *only child syndrome*. When she turned seven, she chose to live on the road with her father and saw her mom on the off seasons, but could have done without it. Our fathers were the best of friends—not that they had a choice with Scarlett's insistence on staying wherever we did. I am not sure if she was ever formally invited to anything, but we soon got used to having a fifth kid around and nobody seemed to mind.

Scarlett's dad was killed in an accident when she was fifteen. Her mother had first right to her but when we asked if she could spend the rest of the season with us, her mother was happy to say yes. Scarlett never ended up going home. Not that it's needed to be said, but my parents cared for Scarlett like their baby-making parts made her themselves.

My parents are true nurturers. Adding Scarlett to our bunch was not even up for debate in my mother's mind. She really loves kids. If my dad hadn't gotten snipped after the fourth, who knows how many of us there would've been? I think they're such good parents because they truly like each other. Rare these days, I know. But what can I say, they are freaks of nature.

Mom and Dad both grew up in separate small towns in the U.S. They met at a Rolling Stones concert in Atlanta in 1978 and got married three weeks later. They were, and still are, sickly in love with each other. Their bond meant that wherever my dad went, we went, and we were grateful for that. We Greens consider ourselves half American and half everything else imaginable. My older sister, Liv, was born in Hockenheim, Germany; I was born in Dijon, France; my younger brother, Charles, was born in Adelaide, Australia, and my little sister, Violet, in Barcelona, Spain. We settled in San Francisco during the off months and had a home in Paris as our hub during the season, though we were hardly ever there. We speak four different languages but understand six, are all talented in the sport of fencing, and are able to distinguish the difference in taste between a Merlot and a Cabernet Sauvignon with our eyes closed.

The lifestyle may sound lavish but don't start thinking we are some snobby rich family only interested in the finer things, because we are far from it. Some may be fooled by our designer attire and flashy cars but the truth is, we all learned how to hunt by the age of ten, prefer bathing in fresh water lakes to fancy showers, and our favorite family dinner is goose. Well, we drink champagne from Champagne, France—the only true Champagne!—and what we learned to hunt is quail, but that is standard.

Okay, so we aren't hillbilly, but I swear we are balanced. Like every child does, I attribute that, and many other abnormal things, to my parents. Our version of balanced is that no matter where we were in the world, or how many mistakes we've all made, what keeps us together is our no-judgment and only unconditional love policy. It really works.

How did I fit into this eccentric assembly? I am known as the entertainer of the bunch. As soon as I learned how to talk, I created my own stories. I would craft these elaborate and strangely detail-oriented tales of siblings from another planet, imaginary friends that could breathe under water, and monsters that braided my hair while I was asleep. Sometimes, my stories included songs, and my incapability to hold a tune would make everyone laugh. I didn't care if they were laughing at me; I just liked making people happy. I was always a quirky little kid, and now I am a quirky petite adult. Some things don't change.

When Scarlett and I got accepted to the University of Cambridge-thanks to Dad and not our grades-we settled into our fabulous flat and melted with the excitement of independence. I would say we were sad to be apart from the family, but I'm pretty sure our attention was solely focused on enjoying our freedom and having fun. We lit up our first cigarette, a habit I never admitted to having; poured ourselves a glass of wine, a habit I openly admit to still having; and set a mission—before our future careers took our social lives away, we would do whatever and whomever we wanted without any regrets.

We never kicked that habit.

At this point, Scarlett and I are both twenty-eight, in the best shape of our lives, and hard-working, kickass chicks. Oh, and single, but not the *awww, poor her* kind of single; more like the *wow, look at them go* kind of unattached.

Scarlett is a fashion photographer and I, proudly, managed to become the successful business owner of a trendy upscale boutique in San Francisco's famous Nob Hill. Our careers fit hand in hand; Scarlett gets the first eye on the hottest new designs and designers, and I get them in my store before anyone else. Let's just say, thanks to a shoot Scar had in Australia, I had Dion Lee in my store before the label even made it to an American runway.

Thanks to being the significant runt of the litter of five-nine-plus tall siblings, my favorite styles of clothing are out of the question. No high-waisted flare pants or long boho dresses for me at five-one and a half. Damn my legs. If only they could grow along with the list of celebrities that shop at my boutique. Unfortunately, that is impossible. Trust me, I've looked into it.

At least my petite stature seems to be a winning size in the eyes of many hunky men. Though Scarlett, who has always been in support of my career, was never as gung-ho about the men that gravitated towards me. The real reason—she gets jealous of the time they take me away from her. Growing up with so many inherited siblings, you'd think she would be better at sharing. She is not.

Every guy I date, I give a real shot to, so I end up investing a lot of time in them at the beginning, which weans out the weak much quicker. To make it through Round One takes a lot more than looks and a bank account. Something more, something unexplainable at the time, has to click. This, to me, is the best dating technique.

I blame my parents for my inherent determination to find my life mate and not just my first husband. Because of that, I think it's better to spend time together to see if you really picture that guy being a part of your team, and not just on your roster.

The problem I've now come across is that the ten men I've let in have kind of stayed in, too.

Chapter Two

Let's Do This

Scarlett snatches the list from my hands and stretches it out in front of her face.

Does she think the names will become clearer the further away she holds it? How precious. Maybe as a joke, I'll buy her some bifocals. She'll be totally miffed at that. It's brilliant. I'll add it to my mental to-do list. I squeeze my eyes shut. Okay, added.

Scarlett waves her hands in front of my eyes to grab my attention. "See Alex, 1, 5, 9, and 10 are all pretty-boys. 3, 4, 6, 7, and 8 were all sorts of muscular, and 2 had a British accent so that was all the appeal he needed. Out of all the places we've traveled, a British accent is still the sexiest."

Well, she's not wrong. There's something in their tone that is so sophisticated and proper, yet made you want to give in and scream *okay, take off my clothes and make messy passionate love to me, already*. Maybe it's just because we both associate the accent with Hugh Grant. Ya, that could very well be it, we're suckers for Rom Coms. "Yes, 9 was pretty but he was crazy when he drank, and he could totally take 4."

She throws her hands in the air. "4 was a recovering addict; my Nona could take him."

"Being off drugs is something we are using in his 'weaknesses' column?" I question as I feel a frown scrunching over my forehead.

She jumps in without hesitation or even the blink of an eye. "Pretty much. Also, in his weakness column is that he was a surfer and they are all emotional. Emotional men make weak fighters."

Playing devil's advocate for no particular reason, I continue to defend him. "Who says that? Some people go crazy serial killer because of their passion. And passion is emotion."

Her tone turns inquisitive. "So who do you think would win in a fight?"

I shrug, not having given this any thought before. I mean, why would I? Not only do I think seeing men fight over a girl is extremely unattractive, but having your exes all meet each other is probably a woman's worst fear. Though, it would get me to stop being so mesmerized by their hot bods. "Out of all of them?"

"Yup." Scarlett tucks the list into her back pocket as she gets up to grab another bottle of wine.

I lean sideways, stretch out my arm out as far as it would possibly go, and just barely, with my index and middle finger, snatch the paper out of her pocket. I look at all ten names as if I could see them materialize before my eyes, then picture each of their faces at our happiest moments. For some reason, this is what my memory chooses to regurgitate at the first thought of them.

Then images of those faces getting punched flitted in, and hysterical laughter bubbled in my throat.

Scarlett must hear me laugh to myself all the way from the kitchen.

"So, if all of them were in one room and had no choice but to fight each other, who do you think would win?" she shouts.

"It isn't that easy for me to think of them fighting each other because I am mostly attracted to lovers, not fighters," I holler back.

"Oh, please," she mumbles just loud enough for me to hear it.

How dare that hussy? It's not like I was lying. Okay, it may have sounded cheesy, but it was true. The second I saw a guy's chest puff out, I ran quickly in the other direction. Who wants to be with someone that possibly has anger management issues? Not me. I may not like fighters, but that doesn't mean I don't like my men strong and fit.

As they materialize in my mind, I line up all ten men side by side like in an episode of the Bachelorette.

Wow, it seems like I do have a type; tall and handsome with great hair. Not bad.

Then, beside each of them appears a list of attributes—some longer than others, of course. I consider their personalities and realize that if they were put in a life or death situation, there would be a few very strong contenders for the win.

Like I naturally do with everything, I take it to the next level. I guess that's due to the ambitious businesswoman in me. Or maybe the thrill seeker—I do have a tendency to enjoy jumping out of planes. After all, no one has ever said excitement is boring, right? So like on the *Choose your warrior* screen of any *Mortal*

Combat-type videogame, I pitted these men one against the other, including variables such as location, weapons, and sheer will. I can feel my eyes growing bigger like a kid watching sprinkles added to their cupcake. Except this is a lot less sweet and a little more insane.

"Let's fight them to the death!" I tell Scarlett when she returns and I jump off the couch.

She looks up at me in surprise. "What? We are actually going to kill them?"

I chuckle. "We won't be getting our hands bloody, but I'm happy to hear you're down to be an accomplice if I ever need one."

She stands with her hands on her hips. "Listen, I'm Italian. I have a body bag in my closet and an uncle who doesn't ask questions on speed dial."

I stare at her for a few seconds. She would make a really great mob boss. I think she's actually tough enough to cut a man's ear off if necessary. She once ate a raw goat heart—so who knows what she's capable of?

Scarlett puts her hand on my shoulder and breaks the silence. "Don't worry, you're family. Vito won't ask you any questions, either."

I'm not sure what to think of that, but I suppose you can never be too certain you won't need these kinds of resources in the future. I'll drop it for now, and probably grab his number later.

Though, she could be on to something here. Obviously, cold-blooded murder is taking it a little, okay a lot, too far, but when wine can no longer solve my problems, maybe an axe can. A metaphorical one, of course. These exes seem to still have a strong hold of my being, since I am able to imagine them so vividly and all. I know I've let them go in my physical state, but possibly not my mental one.

Aha! That's where my chest pain was coming from earlier—my head! Maybe I should take a note from the Uncle Vito handbook and find a way to off these suckers once and for all.

I shuffle towards her with a pep in my step. "Hey Scarface. Maybe I can't break my attachments to my exes because I keep moving on in the traditional way, you know, with another man."

She nods. "Best way to do it. Works every time, for me."

Fuelled by her support, I take a deep breath and finish the thought that just popped up. "But it clearly hasn't worked. Maybe because I'm not exactly a traditional kind of girl. So why not try something weird and twisted? Imagining them die may be the only solution."

Scarlett's eyes grow wide and she beams. "Can we have snipers?"

"We can have snipers." I love how into this she is getting.

She puckers her lips and kisses the air. "Something about a man who knows how to handle a rifle with precision is so sexy to me."

That's the girl I know. Mention one thing that sparks her inner horny old man and any animosity held in our conversation seconds ago is all but forgotten. She's been the same way since she was sixteen. Nothing will distract her faster than a hot guy on a street corner. Which is probably why I'm always nervous being a passenger in her car.

As for me, I blossomed quite late as a woman. I didn't even get boobs until I was seventeen. So when I turned eighteen and started receiving all of this attention from men, I soaked it in like a sponge. My parents are in a sickly perfect relationship so I have always wanted to find what they have. I just didn't realize it was going to be so hard. There are a lot of fucking frogs out there that don't turn into princes when you kiss them. And I've kissed more than a few. I, of course, have standards, but I have this innate ability to see people's potential. Optimism is a bitch.

After I lost my virginity, I basically haven't been single. Once I got my boobs, the rest of my body bloomed into womanhood and boys with muscles and strong jaws started to notice me. It was awesome. Not my fault if I'm desirable. But it *is* my fault that I have a hard time saying no. I always think if my mother had said no to my father, I wouldn't be here. So maybe my optimism has a little bit too much fantasy in it. Yet, I like it that way.

And having boyfriend after boyfriend is not something I regret. I've learned the things I like and don't like; I've learned how I want to be treated; and I've learned that looks don't determine a man's self-confidence. I have experienced hard times, good times, and amazing times. And now, I can tell very quickly if a man is going to be with me in the long run or not. As cliché and eye rolling as it sounds, I believe that everything happens for a reason. If I feel for even one second that something isn't meant to be, I shut off my emotion switch and give them a 'peace out-high five'.

Unfortunately, that hasn't resulted in them being cut out of my heart or mind for good. Maybe the problem that I need to solve in order to move on is to actually feel.

Ugh. Feeling is the worst.

This exercise may be unconventional and a little sadistic, but if it works, man, is it going to be worth it.

My focus snaps back on Scarlett sitting on the couch in front of me as I stand nearly hovering over her.

"Having them metaphorically die is still going to be hard. But I've tried everything from sex therapy to professional therapy and I still have attachments to these ten men. I need to get creative now. I need to regain control of my emotions. So let's set up a metaphorical fight to the death and see what happens."

Scarlett grabs my arm and throws me on the sofa. In a squeak of springs, she mumbles loud enough for me to hear. "It would be more fun if the fight wasn't metaphorical."

I roll onto my side and push my body back to seated position. Her mumble creeps into my ears and the shock slackens my jaw as I gape at her. "What's that? You want to actually murder them?"

She shrugs and gives me a *maybe* look with her raised eyebrows. Then she waves and smiles. "I'm just kidding. I think this will be fun. It is a way for you to be in control of the situation while still being able to take a step back and analyze your feelings." She pauses, as if lost in thought. "Though I don't think it's going to work, but let's try, anyways. I'm up for anything."

That was the truth. She was always up for anything, just ask the multicultural eight on her paper. She even picked one of them up while swimming with sharks. Sure, it was a photo shoot and he was the model, but still, she's done crazier things than imagining a few of my exes dying. Come to think of it, I'd be surprised if she hasn't secretly done that many times. This should be a breeze for her.

"Oh, one more thing," she adds.

"Ya?"

She smoothes her hands along the sides of her long and curvy silhouette. "Can my dress be red? I want to be wearing a red dress while we kill your exes."

Yep. She's definitely thought this up before. Maybe that's a good thing. I'll need all the help I can get.

I snap my fingers. "Done. Your dress is red."

Her eyes light up with excitement. "Let's do this thing, shall we?" Anticipation drips from her tone.

"Done."

I close my eyes and return to the image of the bachelors lined up.

Hello boys, welcome to my twisted thoughts.

Chapter Three

Assemble The Troops

The sun has started to set, the warm summer breeze cool at this time of the evening. One by one, the men arrive at the exclusive rooftop lounge of the Theodore hotel in Los Angeles.

None of them recognize each other at first glance or have any idea why they have been summoned to this event, but all attend without hesitation.

A long-legged hostess hands each attendee a glass of champagne and brings to their attention the names inscribed on the lounge furniture.

Organized side by side in the shape of a half circle facing the extravagant glass bar in the middle of the rooftop, ten names are prominently engraved on ten oversized, posh designer black leather *Prouvé*'s Cité lounge chairs.

The men take their designated seats and wait in cautious silence.

Three seconds later, Tommy, the salt-and–pepper-haired, thirty-two-year-old boy in a man's body, downs his glass of champagne and walks up to the hostess. "You got whisky up in here?"

She stares at the rooftop bar, stacked four glass shelves high. "You must be Number 9, the classy one."

He raises his eyebrows in confusion, making his big blue eyes almost too large, then gets distracted like a puppy with a treat as the double shot of whisky lands on the counter. The eyebrows and eyes return to normal. He takes the shot, gets another, and returns to his seat.

The man to his left looks at him with disgust and disappointment but opens his mouth to say, " Atta boy".

That is classic Number 10: Clint, a thirty-seven-year-old successful Hollywood-based celebrity lawyer and permanent bachelor. He is six-foot-two, has a slim figure and slicked-back blond hair, which tells everyone he means business. He is social, ambitious, dapper, sophisticated, smart, and fashionably conscious. Also very silly, with the sense of humor of a five-year-old.

Metro-sexual and immature isn't usually my type, but he is hard to hate. He is so suave he wins the hearts of every person—woman or man—he meets. He also has the most mischievous smile with dimples that make you forgive him for anything he does.

From day one, I saw straight through him. How? Well, when he walked into my boutique, chasing around one of his celebrity clients, I immediately noticed his number one character flaw: his need to fit in. Even if he completely despises someone's personality, he will be extremely friendly and even pretend to have things in common with them, in front of their faces. Behind their back, of course, he will judge the shit out of them and try to avoid being around them again at all costs. I saw it in action that day, when he commented enthusiastically as his client tried on my entire vintage Yves St. Laurent collection. But as soon as she tucked back behind the curtain, his hand went on his head, rubbing his temples. When she popped back out, he was Mr. Happy again. Of course, people hardly ever realized his flaw because they were too busy being mesmerized by his very convincing acting skills and chiseled jaw. He made one damn good lawyer.

Clint gazes with his pale blue eyes around the rooftop with extreme skepticism. He is the first to wonder *who are all of these people? Why am I here?* And fittingly, *are there networking opportunities?* He sizes up the crowd, noticing only ten people and one hostess whom he does not recognize but is visualizing naked. He does a double take on Number 8, Sebastian, a twenty-nine-year-old eccentric entrepreneur he met at a conference in Berlin a few years back.

Sebastian is six feet four inches tall and over two hundred pounds of solid German muscle. His shoulders are as wide as my car, which also happens to be German. He is wise beyond his years, a very successful businessman, and the oddest person I have ever known. We met at a rooftop lounge in Frankfurt, much like this one. I was intrigued when he confidently approached me and told me he was an assassin. I immediately decided not to take him seriously but instead be amused by his strangeness. Later that evening, he joked and said he was getting bored with our conversation and asked if I would like to find other people to talk to, with him. His peculiar humor and behavior made me laugh the hardest I have ever laughed. After six months of sporadic dates, I broke his heart without knowing he ever had one.

Clint walks up to Sebastian and reaches out his hand for an intimidating handshake. Sebastian counters with an aggressive glare into Clint's eyes. A match made in egocentric heaven.

"Hi, Sebastian Krause, right? We met in Berlin at the Strategic Business Development conference. How are you?"

"We never met", Sebastian responds. "I was a speaker, though, so you obviously remember me. No one else I've ever met has the capability to captivate and enlighten a crowd such as me."

Unimpressed with his overt narcissism but unsure how to respond, Clint takes a sip of his champagne.

"I'm just fucking with you, buddy. It's Clint Tate, right?" Sebastian jokes as he delivers a harder than expected pat to Clint's shoulder.

The tension eases and both simultaneously run their fingers in their hair to smooth out their blond coifs.

"You know, I am glad to see a familiar face. Do you have any idea why we are here?" Clint asks.

"I hope it's to develop some sort of A-team or secret society," Sebastian fantasizes.

Clint starts to hum out the A-team theme song "Ba, da da, dun dun dun..." Sebastian joins in and brings up his arm for a testosterone charged high-five.

The chumminess between 8 and 10 encourages the others to converse.

Number 4, Rob, a thirty-one-year-old ex pro-surfer who not only looked, but also acted, exactly like Tarzan, walks up to Tommy/ Mr. Whisky, Number 9 and offers him his glass of champagne.

Rob is six-foot-two, chiseled from his jaw to his ankles, strong, wise, talks like a dumb surfer, and cries more than my little sister after losing a game of Monopoly.

Putting his champagne glass in Tommy's face, Rob offers, "Yo bud, want my glass? My sponsor would be mega bummed if I broke. Sweet-fizz has never been my poison so here you go, dude."

Tommy's eyebrows rise again. "I have no idea what you just said, but ya, I'll drink it, thanks man." He takes the glass and chugs it without hesitation.

Rob reaches his arm out and rests it on Tommy's shoulder. "Have you thought about joining the program?"

Tommy spontaneously bursts into screaming. "Is this what this stuffy, fucking party is about? Some sort of intervention? Well, fuck you all! I don't have a problem and I refuse to be judged like this. Everyone should mind their own fucking business and get their own lives."

The whole crowd stops and watches to see what he will do next.

Tommy kicks over his large leather lounge chair and walks with his chest puffed out towards the exit.

Tommy is no stranger to the level I like to call "red-zone." He is not one of my finer moments in dating history, and not only because he is thirty-two and still calls himself Tommy. We met at a bar one night when I was out with the girls. In Vegas. He was the bartender. All red flags, I know. But we had a great few months together partying and just hanging out. It was fun, comfortable, and easy.

Then it became difficult, childish, and frustrating. I soon realized he was like a heartbroken teenage boy. He drank way too much all the time and was always looking for a fight-even at my work events. The line was always there; he just never saw it, and definitely did not mind crossing it. He would come over to my place in LA on weekdays with random scrapes and bruises all over his body that he collected over the weekend, but never knew where they came from. After a few conversations with his friends and family, I found out he wasn't over his ex, whose picture was still on his bedside table—yes, I know: another red flag. What can I say? I was being stubborn. But after five months, I had enough. I walked into his bar, wasn't surprised to see him flirting with another girl, and called it quits right then and there. Yes, it was a bit dramatic, but damn did it feel good.

Startled by the temper tantrum, surfer Rob begins to sob. He is an overly sensitive and overtly emotional guy. He once cried when we were out snorkeling together because he saw two turtles swimming so close to each other that it looked like they were holding hands.

Walking with purpose towards Rob is Number 7, Matteo, a thirty-two-year-old

Roman carpenter and manly man. He is only five feet nine inches tall but he is built completely of muscle. On his time off, he goes to the gym, plays video games, collects ancient weapons, buys guns and crossbows for hunting, and only watches action-filled movies. He is a passionate man, a religious man, a proud man, a secure man, a respectful man, an honest and a loyal man. Also a man of few words, but the words he speaks have meaning to them. He holds the people close to him with high regard and great respect, yet, truly feels that he is often taken for granted. He is the first person people think of when they need a hand around the house, but not when they're planning a dinner party, so he's probably right.

"You have to stop crying. You are a man and men do not cry because it shows weakness. Do you want these gentlemen to think you are weak? No," Matteo quietly but firmly preaches into Rob's ear.

Rob stops crying, stands up a little straighter, and apologizes for his minor breakdown. "I'm sorry. I'm Rob. I'm a recovering addict and it really, you know, troubles me when I see people suffering and not accepting help and kindness."

"Hi, Rob. I'm Matteo." He firmly shakes the sad surfer's hand. "First, do not apologize to me unless it is warranted. Stop feeling sorry for yourself. We all have our demons but you should never reveal them to complete strangers. You are a fit, young, and good-looking man; you should find yourself a woman who will take care of you and build up your confidence. A man is like a house and women are the foundation. A firm foundation is the basis for every solidly built structure. Find that and you will be complete."

Matteo waits seven seconds for a reaction from Rob.

Rob stares back, stunned. "Dude, that is so deep. I have so much to learn from you."

As Matteo becomes Rob's new mentor, across the room, unable to open the exit door, stands red flag Tommy, frustrated to the max. He turns to the closest man, grabs his blazer, and shouts, "Why?"

Unfortunately, he grabbed Number 2, Henry.

Henry is a twenty-nine-year-old tattooed, northern British retired (injured-not on the field) rugby player that stands at a towering six feet six inches and whose mentor is UK's bad-boy rocker, Pete Doherty. He is goofy yet arrogant, loving yet condescending, incredibly smart yet un-ambitious, and athletic yet lazy. His favorite past-time is drinking beer and he has the emotional stability of a drunk college boy.

"Oy, mate, push off," Henry shouts back.

Tommy lets go and takes a step back.

Henry is not done, though. "I don't know why, but I sure as shit haven't the first idea of who you are, lad. So stop mucking about, you're embarrassing yourself."

"So this isn't an intervention?" Tommy asks.

"Aren't those things with family?" Henry questions.

Relief floods Tommy. "Oh, thank fuck. Sorry about that, bud. Let's get a shot, what do you say?"

"Fuckin' right. You're a crazy little muppet but I like you. I'm Henry." He extends his arm for a complicated secret-like handshake.

Tommy doesn't follow. It becomes awkward. They digress and head to the bar.

At the bar, enjoying a pint of beer, is Number 1, Chad, a twenty-seven-year–old, six-foot-tall guitarist with the face of a baby and the body of a cocaine addict. Despite being covered in tattoos and sporting a stylish but loud Mohawk, Chad is not your conventional obnoxious rocker; he has never tried drugs and is one of the shyest guys I know. He carries a hard shell around that is virtually impossible to crack and get in. But when he drops his guard for you, it is well worth the wait and effort.

He sits at the bar in silence, observing and evaluating each person. He knows no one and therefore he interacts with no one. But he listens.

He hears Henry and Tommy heading towards the bar while discussing their favorite Premier League teams.

"Glory for the Gunners is all," Henry proclaims.

"Arsenal is my team, too!" Tommy anxiously shares.

Almost immediately, the two burst into song. " Arsenal, we're on your side, Our love we can not hide…"

They approach the bar, where Tommy orders two pints and Henry continues on. "…Our hearts are open wide, To cheer you along the way, We will be standing by…"

Henry moves over to Chad and wraps his arm around him like they are old mates. "We know how hard you try, Whether you win or lose"

Henry then jumps around the bar, gets down on one knee before the hostess, and serenades her with the rest. "It's you that we choose, So special when youse around."

She blushes, then laughs. "British accent, tall and lanky, charming but obnoxious. You must be Henry."

Without questioning her on-point knowledge of him, he kisses her hand. "The pleasure is all mine, m'lady."

As silly as it seems, this is the charm I fell for. Typical, I know. The fact that he has no shame in showing who he is at all times was refreshing and extremely entertaining. We met in university. He was certainly not your typical Cambridge student. He was one of its star rugby athletes, but his piss poor attitude made every coach and professor despise him. But for some reason, that just made his peers like him more. Uni environments are complicated. I can't blame myself for being gullible and naive then. My reasoning-everyone goes through a Henry phase at least once, don't they?

Standing near the ledge, taking in the view from the fortieth floor while nursing his first glass of champagne and creating a picture worthy of a GQ cover, is the ever-dapper Number 6, Liam.

Liam was a thirty-four-year-old successful pharmaceutical executive from Sydney, Australia. He was six feet two inches, an absolute gentleman, wealthy, suave, and built like a brick house. He was raised by a single mother, which makes him both responsible and sweet. His father was American, not that he ever knew him, though. He moved to San Francisco with his mother and twin sisters when he was fifteen. He has unfortunately outgrown his accent, but not the adorable freckles on his nose. He has a golden, verging on red, full head of hair that fell just perfectly no matter what situation or time of day. As successful as he is in business today, his dream was always to be in the ballet.

Liam turns to his right and sees someone smoking a cigarette in the corner. He walks over. "Hey, I'm Liam. Weird party, right? You mind if I bum a smoke off you?"

"Hey, Liam. I'm Alec. This isn't a cigarette, it's a joint, but you are welcome to some if you like," Number 3 answers.

Oh, Number 3, I say while sighing. That is Alec, a twenty-eight-year-old professional American football player of Croatian descent. The man was not made with brains but dear Jesus, is he beautiful. He resembles a Greek God and makes love like one would, too. He is six-foot–two-inches tall, strong, manly, and a legitimate athlete. His dark hair and eyes create this mysteriousness about him that makes anyone who meets him melt. He ends up in most of those women's beds.

"Ya, sure, why not." Liam accepts as Alec passes the dutchie on the left-hand side. He inhales and coughs uncontrollably while exhaling.

Alec starts to laugh. "There you go, it's been a while, hasn't it? Feels good, right? It will definitely make this PR event more fun."

"What do you mean, PR event?" Liam questions as he regains control of his lungs and hands the joint back to Alec.

"I got this text saying to come here tonight and not ask questions. I usually get those from my agent. I've agreed to do as he says since the last incident," Alec reveals.

Liam takes a step back, his mind a little foggy but his body more relaxed than ever. He opens his eyes as wide as he can. "Holy shit, you're Alec Lonza. You're the star quarterback for the Alabama Tigers. That's been my favorite team since I was a little kid because my Dad is from the South. Not that I knew him, but I've always imagined he would like the Tigers. I remember your rookie year when you guys won the Super Bowl. What an insane year it must have been for you. Sorry I am rambling, I get like that when I'm high."

Alec nods. "That's alright, dude. Always great to meet a reporter who is also a fan. Bad press bums me out."

Liam clarifies, "No, no, I'm not a reporter. I don't think this is a PR thing. I'm a Pharmaceutical Executive."

Confusion glows on Alec's face even more. "So why are we here and how long do we have to stay? I'm going to get the munchies soon."

Liam jumps in with passion. "Wait, you thought this was a PR thing for you and you were smoking pot? Are you aware how stupid that is? You are so young and talented. Your agent lets you do this? You need better representation."

A few feet away, new BFFs Clint and Sebastian hear the word "representation" and rush over to Alec and Liam. When they realize who Alec is, their eyes light up, and if you look close enough, you could probably see money signs in their pupils.

Sitting alone, still in his designated lounge chair, is the last man to introduce himself to the group, Number 5, Josh. Josh is a thirty-year-old professional European football referee who was my first true love, and I his. He is a diamond-in-the-rough kind of charmer from a family of six in Ireland. He is the only boy. For some reason, having five sisters made me like him more-as if that would confirm he would treat me better than someone without five sisters. How silly.

He lived in LA for five years and stuck out like a sore thumb. Not because he sounded like Colin Farrell but because he didn't like glitz or glam, parties or movies. He just liked football (or soccer, as us North Americans know it by). He was there to get work as a referee to build up a reputation before going back to the UK. He is six-feet tall, very fit, had a smile that could melt a room, and eyes like a wolf. His curly brown hair has a little blond streak in it on the left side of his head, just over his ear. He always wanted to die it brown, but I loved it just the way it was.

Josh's biggest flaw is his lack of confidence and trust. It completely consumed him to the point where he would develop a Jeckyl and Hyde type of persona. He is an asshole one second and the sweetest man in the world the next. He is insecure in himself and because of that, every person or thing that was near me threatened him. Yikes, right? Well, we can't always learn our lessons the easy way.

Josh gets up from his seat to see what the commotion is all about at the balcony. He approaches Alec, Liam, Clint, and Sebastian. "Hey guys, what's up? I'm Josh. Does anyone know what the heck we're doing here? It's been over an hour. I thought I was here for a UEFA announcement."

Clint is the first to shake his hand, holding eye contact until Josh breaks. Sebastian fights Liam for the second introductory handshake.

While Sebastian is busy trying to be more intimidating than Clint, Liam responds to Josh. "Hi Josh, nice to meet you. It's funny you mention that, because Alec also thought this was a sports-related PR event. We don't think it is. Clint, Sebastian, and I aren't athletes; just Alec is."

"Oh, you're a footballer, Alec? What team do you play for?" Josh asks, accentuating his Irish twang.

Alec puffs his chest out. "Ya, I am. Play for the Alabama Tigers."

Josh squints with confusion and smiles as he always does when Americans get the two football sports mixed up. Then his face starts to look flushed and his heart drops to his feet as he realizes who Alec is.

When Josh and I were living together in Los Angeles, before he got the contract with UEFA as a referee, he was refereeing children's games in California and his pride would feel bruised every now and then when he reminded himself I once dated a professional athlete. Though he knew it wasn't the same sport, he still felt inferior to Alec. He would see him on TV and immediately get furious. I am convinced he was more jealous of Alec's success than our past relationship. Even so, I would steer clear of watching all sports and eventually TV in general, in hopes to avoid Josh seeing Alec. His insecurity was purely self-inflicted and there was rarely anything I could say or do to calm him down. Usually when he got mad, I would give him a few minutes to calm down from red-zone, remind him I loved him and have been with him faithfully and willingly for years. On good days, he would apologize, I would nod, and we would go about our day. This went on until the day I left him.

"You're Alec Lonza. Nice to meet you, man," Josh politely responds and finally acts like a mature adult.

Alec shakes his hand.

Josh doesn't let go and holds onto his hand tighter and tighter.

High as a kite, Alec starts to laugh uncontrollably. "Hey man, can I have my hand back? This thing makes me a lot of money."

A fake laugh escapes each of their mouths.

Shaking out of his rage and letting go of Alec's hand, Josh nods. "Sorry, I guess I just have so much pent up unnecessary anger towards you. You dated my ex."

Alec waves his words off. "That's alright; you're not the first guy to be pissed I dated their girl. I dated a lot of girls who were bummed about their exes." He smirks. "Or even girls who were bummed about their current men."

Alec turns to Sebastian who happily supports him with a high five.

Josh corrects him. "No, she dated you before me, I just always hated having to live up to you, but I guess we are both in the same position now, without her, so it seems silly to dwell".

"I dated her before? Like, when before?" Alec asks.

Josh thinks for a second, then recalls. "Your rookie year, I think."

Liam jerks his head backwards in shock. "Whoa, your ex dated him the year he won the Super Bowl? No wonder you hated him. No one can compare to that."

"I know, right?" Josh exclaims while he laughs.

Clint joins in on the laughter even though he was not present in the conversation, but gives Josh a supportive man-pat on the back, anyways.

Liam, Sebastian, Josh, and Clint all laugh while Alec stands still with his head down. This is what he does when he is trying to think. Needless to say, it is a blessing and shock to most that Alec can act fast on the field, probably because he doesn't have time to think.

Alec raises his head. "Is your ex Vanessa?"

Correcting him, Josh says, "No, her name was Alexandria."

Chapter Four

The Guys Know

Liam takes a step back and watches the room. He and I are still friends so he wonders why I didn't tell him about this night. Acting overly paranoid, he pulls out his cell and tries to call me. His phone doesn't work. The room, to him, starts spinning as he realizes he has, in fact, heard of each of these men before.

During our relationship, Liam and I were always better friends than we were lovers. We would go out dancing for hours, secretly smoke pot together, share stories about our recently failed relationships, dreams, aspirations, and began to care about each other-in a big brother, little sister kind of way. One day at an event we attended with many other friends, he admitted to me why there was no romantic spark between us—I met his ex-fiancée whom he hated, and I was her doppelganger. We laughed about it for ages. The romance died out after just two months but the friendship remained.

Liam takes another step back to balance himself against the ledge. He focuses his vision and starts looking around the room.

Henry continues to hit on the leggy hostess; Tommy chugs yet another pint of beer; Chad remains content and quiet, avoiding all eye contact with the other men; Rob willingly listens to Matteo's words of wisdom; while Josh, Alec, Clint, and Sebastian start putting the "Alexandria" pieces together.

Sebastian steps out of the crowd, storms to the middle of the rooftop, and shouts with his big gorilla arms in the air. "Who here knows Alexandria Green?"

Everyone stops what they're doing and looks at Sebastian. One by one, each guy raises his hand.

Chad stands up, holds his head high, and speaks for the first time. "I was Alexandria's first."

Henry stands up straight, pushes the hostess over while trying to get out from behind the bar, walks up to Chad, and defensively states, "I was Alex's first, lad, so she couldn't have been yours."

Yes, I may have let Number 2, Henry, think he was number 1, but in my defense, I didn't really consider it a lie because he was, in fact, the first to make me climax. I realize that is not what constitutes a sexual partner but for some reason, at the time, the lie came out of my mouth to Henry and I had to stick with it. It was actually Number 3, Alec, that showed me the light, and by light, I mean an unbelievable orgasm, correction, multiple orgasms. I wouldn't see that kind of light again until Number 8, Sebastian.

Wise man Matteo walks over to the overly heated Henry and gently pulls him away from Chad's space. "Does a number really matter now after all these years? We should all just be lucky we had the chance to have her in our lives. Sure, she was quirky, sarcastic as hell, and a little sexist towards women, but she was one of the best girls I've ever dated and I'm sure everyone here would agree."

As Henry backs away from Chad's face, Josh walks towards Matteo with hostility and defensively shouts, "Who are you to think you have the right to be telling us about Ally…"

I hated when he called me that.

"...She was the love of my life. I was going to marry her. The day she left me, she ripped my heart out, froze it in her ice queen hands, and crushed it to pieces. To imagine any of you thinking you have or had feelings for her makes me fucking sick to my stomach. No one knows her like I know her. No one will ever love her like I loved her. She was the best girl I've ever met, not one of the best, but *the* best."

Josh takes a deep breath after his passionate rant, nervously runs his hands through his dark brown, Adrian Grenier haircut, and walks towards the bar, pissed off.

Liam follows and puts his arm around Josh with the intention of comforting the heartbroken hero. "Hey Josh, I'm not sure if it matters to you, but Alexandria and I are friends and she only ever talks about you with a smile on her face."

Josh calms down and smiles. "She talks about me? Really?"

While Liam and vodka on the rocks console Josh and the rest of the guys introduce themselves to each other, the hostess grabs her cell phone and sends the text, "It's time."

Chapter Five

Alexandria Is Here

The sun has set, the floor lights brighten beneath their feet, and the canopy lights turn on to give the effect of floating luminescence ten feet above their heads. The men look down then up like a kitten chasing a laser.

The hostess comes out from behind the bar and walks towards the exit. Every man's eyes follow the olive-skinned, bodacious blonde as her hips shake side to side through the crowd. She gets to the door, looks back, puts her finger in front of her mouth, purses out her lips, and says "Shhhhhhhh".

Wearing pale platform heels, the tightest white *Hervé Léger* mini dress I could think of, my dark brown hair waved and whisping over my shoulders, lips glossed and eyes smoky, I enter through the metal rooftop door, lift my head, turn it slightly to the right, look at all the men, and smile.

I look great, though my breath isn't the best as I just puked ten minutes ago from being so insanely nervous. After all, I am about to address an entire room filled with my exes. That is a scary thought to any girl.

I shyly but cutely say, "Hey, guys" while continuing to tilt my head sideways. They can't get mad at me if I'm being cute—it's the puppy law.

I break the cute façade and head right into the cool chick version of myself.

"Wow, impressive guys. It only took you ninety-three minutes to figure out who brought you here. Good thing I dated some men with brains or this would have gone on a lot longer, and really, I'm quite anxious to get this started."

Okay, so my nerves are getting to me a little bit as I fidget with my dainty gold bracelet and keep crossing then uncrossing my legs while standing.

The guys wait anxiously in silence for me to explain further. I glance over at Alec who seems to already be disinterested in the conversation as he is staring right beside me at the hostess' breasts.

I decide to refocus him. "Alec, it is you who I am most impressed with. First and foremost for remembering the name Vanessa, who is in fact the mother of your child and whom you cheated on me with in your rookie year. So, good job on that."

Alec smiles and lifts his head with pride, not realizing I was being sarcastic.

I had digressed, and decide to formally address the group, who are all staring directly at me. Incredibly intimidating. I have to break the intensity.

"Good evening, everyone. Looking very dapper tonight. Well, some of you, not all of you, especially not you Tommy. What are you doing with a *Van Halen* t-shirt under your blazer? And Henry, really, white sneakers with a suit? Come on."

As I get a laugh from everyone but Henry and Tommy, I feel like I regained enough power to continue confidently. "Other than that, the rest of you clean up quite well and are looking exceptionally handsome."

Rob shouts awkwardly, "You look handsome, too, Alexandria". Rob looks over at Matteo who shoots back with a charitable, approving wink.

I give him a benign smile before turning to the group again. "As you have all realized by now, it was me that invited you here tonight. You are the elite who have been chosen…"

Whispering in the background, Sebastian looks over at Clint. "A-team, I knew it!" They get closer and do a not-so-subtle fist-bump.

I roll my eyes and continue, "…who have been chosen by me while identifying my exes. I have dated some of you longer than others, but tonight, you remain equals. All of you hold a special part of my past and the past is something I have been holding on to for too long. So tonight is my way of letting you go."

I take a deep breath, look around the room, and start to feel tears well up in my eyes. Seeing them again is harder than I thought it would be. There were some tough moments I went through with a few of these guys. I wave fresh air onto my face. *Get it together, Alexandria; you can do this*-I repeat over and over. I tend to do that quite often; something my dad taught me to help stay focused and keep my head in the game.

As my convincing mantra starts to kick in, my tear ducts begin to dry and Matteo takes a few steps towards me.

"Alexandria, can we talk now? It is great to see you, less great to see all the guys you've slept with..."

Fair enough.

"...but I have wondered how you've been all these years and what I would say to you if I ever saw you again."

He takes another step towards me.

I take one back.

He continues. "But all I can think of right now is that you still have my Blue-Ray player."

Overhearing the conversation, the guys laugh.

I smile and shake my head. "Well, Matteo, thank you for that. It was touching."

Clint raises his hand slightly and says with hesitation, "I believe you also have my golf clubs."

Then, like at a parent-teacher meeting, everyone chimes in at once.

"You have my Red Hot Chili Peppers CD," Chad quietly announces.

"You have my favorite sweater," Tommy accuses.

"You have all of our surf trip pics," Rob adds.

"You have my bread-maker," Liam remembers.

"You have my cat," Sebastian confirms.

"You have my lucky underwear," Alec shouts.

"You have my tool-set, including my drill," Josh recalls.

"You have our sex-tape," Henry proudly proclaims.

I can feel a frown develop between my brows, but only for a moment before laughter begins to bubble inside my throat. Unable to control it, I let out a loud "Ha!"

My body instantly jerks my hand up towards my mouth, trying to stop any more laughter from escaping. It's time to act a little bit more mature.

"Okay, okay, first of all, there is a time limit on some of this stuff. If you don't pick it up in the first three months, it will then belong to me. Standard rule."

A rule that I may have made up, but it makes sense so I'm sticking with it. "Henry, that movie has been deleted a long time ago.

Alec, I definitely don't have your underwear. And Sebastian, that cat was a birthday gift, she is staying with me." Frustrated, I throw my hands in the air. "None of this will matter after tonight is over."

"Alexandria Lou Green," Josh pleads. "I've changed. I want to be able to prove that to you. Don't let me go. I love you, moopy."

I hated when he called me that, too.

"Keep my tools, I don't need them. I need you." He laughs a little then continues. "You are the perfect fit to every nook; if I could be with you for the rest of my life, I would be complete."

I pound my hand to my chest as a slice of pain rips into my heart like a bolt of lightning through an old oak tree. He was always good at brewing up a storm.

"I think my heart may have some feeling in it after all," I joke. "Josh, you know how I feel about you, but our relationship was, and still is, very unhealthy."

I address every man. "I need to be able to move on with my life and I can't do that when I still feel attachments to each of you."

I then man up and switch to the hard-shelled dude side of my personality—the side some men prefer. It makes them feel like I'm their buddy, which I am, for the most part. "This is getting more and more difficult so I am going to try and rip this off like a Band-Aid..."

I pause, take a step backwards and ask the hostess to open the door.

Standing next to the exit, I quickly and arrogantly-on purpose-explain the evening's real purpose.

"Seeing all of this yummy talent in one room, I have to say, it's making me a little sad to announce this next part. For the sole purpose of my amusement, you are all here tonight to fight to the death. As soon as the hostess and I step out, the door will lock behind us. If you try to escape, the snipers positioned on every surrounding building will kill you. There are no other rules. It was a pleasure knowing all of you. Good luck."

Trying not to look at any of them in the face, I follow the hostess through the exit and lock it behind us.

I turn and place my hands on the closed door. The cold steel echoes that of my heart.

The threat of tears sends trembles to my chin. I allow myself to lose control for a moment and melt down. The splash of my tears hit the concrete floor sounding like a gong on my eardrum. I watch each one slam into the ground as they get louder and louder. One, two, three, four, five, six.

That's enough.

On a long inhale, I stand up straight, let my hands off the door, and turn to the hostess as she says, "Well, you look great."

I smile. "Scarlett, take off that ridiculous wig, you know how I feel about blondes. Let's go get some wine and watch this match from the lounge."

With our arms linked, we walk down the stairs in our six-inch heels. We startle at the banging on the door behind us.

We look at each other, smile, then push through the doors to the thirty-ninth floor.

"The fight has begun."

Chapter Six

The Fight Has Begun

Number 5, Josh, runs up to the door as it closes, the look in his eyes divulging his fear that this may be the last time he will ever see me. Tears run down his face in a heartbreaking realization that love sometimes isn't enough.

Then his Hyde comes out. He smashes his glass on the floor and shouts, "You fucking bitch!" He raises his fists in the air and repeatedly hits the steel door. "Ally, don't fucking do this to me! Alexandria, you can't do this to me!"

He breaks down and puts his head in between his legs while he feels every emotion possible rush through his body like a tidal wave.

The rest of the men all gather near the bar counter. Tommy steps into the middle of the crowd, as if to take charge. "Okay guys, you all better fucking listen to me. This bitch is bluffing. I don't see any snipers. I say we get someone to check out how to scale down the wall and maybe get into a window of another floor."

Clint, a natural leader, decides to take over. "This isn't Mission Impossible, Tommy. We don't have any equipment, and unless someone was recently bit by a spider and can now scale walls, it's a death trap. Let's think about this rationally."

Sebastian sees his chance to overstep and counters. "We *are* in a death trap, Clint, don't you get it? Now, I say we split up–"

Chad interrupts with a nerve-stricken shaky hand. "Splitting up is how people die in horror movies."

Sebastian ignores him. "…I say we split up to be able to do some recon of each side of this building. Look for ways to escape. This includes ledges, pipes, other buildings, power lines, anything."

Matteo nods. "Solid plan, Sebastian. While you do that, I will search around the room for materials we can use that would help us to safely exit either over the ledge, to the next building, or through this steel door."

Josh remains crouched next to the door, and Matteo starts ripping the leather off the couches to test its durability while the rest of the men disperse to all four corners of the rooftop.

They spend a few minutes assessing their options and head back to the middle of the room. Josh and Matteo join them.

Sebastian starts. "Okay, on the North side, it is too far to be able to jump to the next building. There aren't any drain pipes. Only small, spaced-out window sills. Considering we are on the fortieth floor, it is unlikely any of us would be able to balance ourselves on those ledges without the wind knocking us over. Henry, what did you find on the West side?"

Henry comes forth. "Alright, well, it's a bloody long ways down and nothing I could see to help that out, but I only got so close. You weren't 'bout to see me go arse over tip. It's quite a hairy situation, if you know what I mean."

Sebastian shakes his head. "Nope. Not sure anyone knows what you mean."

Clint ignores the arrogance and moves the conversation along. "On the South side, the closest building is of greater height than this one, but Chad and I looked over the ledge far enough to see that the nearest window is about ten feet away."

Liam joins in. "On the East side, there's a drainage pipe. Rob thinks it is about a surf board's length from the window, so if we can get someone lean and strong to climb down the pipe, we might have a chance."

Matteo nods. "Excellent. I brought down some of the canopy lights, which we can use as safety rope to assist the climber. We can also use the leather I stripped from the chairs as a harness. The material is impressively strong. Now, to break the window we need to find something heavy that we can throw from ten feet high and will swing into the pane, hopefully not breaking the rope and plummeting forty stories down on to some poor souls."

Josh pats Matteo's back. "Good job, buddy."

Josh, feeling much better after getting some hope of being able to leave here and see me again, decides to take part in the action plan and assertively says, "Matteo and I will tie some of the wood panels from the leather couches together and add sharp instruments to one side, hoping these will penetrate the glass."

Wanting to be a part of Matteo's team, Rob volunteers to help construct the wrecking ball.

Clint takes over and wraps up the plan. "Okay, so Josh, Rob, and Chris will take care of that. Now who will our climber be? I think it should be Chad. Sebastian and Liam are too bulky, Henry has an injured leg, Alec is high, and Tommy is drunk."

Everyone agrees to send Chad over the ledge, except Chad.

"I don't think I should. I'm not the climbing type", shy Chad confirms.

Tommy puts his arm around Chad. "You got this, bud. You're going to do great. It will only take a few minutes and then it will all be over." He leans closer and whispers into Chad's ear. "Do it, or I'll beat the shit out of you." He delivers a hard pat to Chad's chest and walks over to Matteo who is almost finished tying up the harness.

Matteo heads towards Chad. "Your decision to do this makes me proud to have met you." He straps Chad into the harness and ties it tight.

In a last-ditch effort to not be peer-pressured into doing this, Chad pipes up. "Don't you guys think it would be a good idea to break the window first, so I have somewhere to enter when I get down there?"

"Yes, good idea," Matteo concludes then hollers at Josh and Rob. "How much longer until the wrecking ball is all tied up?"

Rob quickly answers, "One minute, boss."

Chapter Seven

I See You

One floor down, Scarlett and I take a seat in our private penthouse lounge and delicately sip a delectable glass of Merlot. Pinkies up.

The 360-degree view of the city offers a stunning and nostalgic experience dazzling any guest on the thirty-ninth floor of the Theodore Hotel in LA.

The black-tiled floor doesn't seem so dark with the impressively expensive, silver-leafed ceiling and all-white modern furniture. Every stylish piece in this chic space remains empty of human company. Except for ours. In the middle of the room, two white contemporary versions of the chaise longue lay under our elongated, slim figures.

We anxiously watch the events on the rooftop unfold as six different cameras allow us to see and hear everything that is happening—in high definition-from the seventy-inch flat screen in front of us.

"It has been fifteen minutes and no one is dead yet," Scarlett observes.

Someone is getting impatient. Did she think this exercise was going to be over in just a few moments? It's not like I can simply imagine them, then bang-bang they're all dead. Over it. Moved on. Ready for a hubby now. No. If cutting my emotional ties to them were that easy, my roommate would be my future husband, not my clingy best friend. I'm going to go through this at my own pace. If this is going to work, I have to make it as close as possible to what would happen in real life.

"Well, I didn't date a bunch of assassins, Scar. They are decent human beings; they will try to escape safely first. Naturally."

She blows a breath into her bangs. "They are being safe, alright! They are building a giant ball of wood as a team."

"They are an innovative gang." By innovative, I mean handy. A combo of athletes and businessmen isn't going to be inventing the world's first successful teleporting machine or anything. But they'd sure look good trying. There's something about manual labor that turns me on. It's probably the sweaty muscle aspect. Or maybe it's the thought of being taken care of. I kind of miss having a man around to handle burnt-out light bulbs and clogged drains.

My butt slides down the chaise longue as a slouch begins to form through my spine. My chin curls into my chest as a result and I catch myself twisting the bottom of my lower lip—a nervous habit I do whenever thinking about something I miss.

For a moment, the private lounge dissolves and we are back in our living room in Nob Hill. My slouch is still evident, the posh lounge chair, not. But I like our big and comfy, beige micro-suede sofa just as much. Though it's a bitch to get wine stains out of.

Scarlett gently places her ruby drink on our coffee table in front of her, sits back, crosses one leg over the other and lays her perfectly manicured hands on top of her knee. This could only mean one thing; it's serious-talk time.

"Alexandria, this is supposed to be a fun fight, but I can tell it means more to you than that. You loved some of these men. You are having a hard time getting to the meat of the fight because you are afraid. Afraid of how you will feel if you do let them go. You need to release your attachments to them, Alex. You owe it to yourself to move on and be happy, and you owe it to your future great love so he is able to have your whole heart, and not just a part of it."

Her words hit me like a ton of bricks. The warm thoughts of my exes lingering in my body and mind all these years have become a part of me. I've gotten too comfortable with having them there, treating them like a security blanket. What do I really have to be afraid of? I already broke up with these guys once. I need to move forward fearlessly. It's time to take off my training bra and woman-up.

I place my hand firmly on Scarlett's knee and look her straight in the eyes. "You're right. I am so glad I have you here for this."

She straightens her back up, matches my gaze with pride and determination in her eyes, and clutches my hand in her firm grasp. Like a coach pumping up a team in every comeback-kid football movie, she gives the motivating talk. "Alexandria Lou Green, you can do this! Man up and let's get back to the fight."

My posture returns to perfection and my mind is clear with its intention.

I don't need a safety blanket anymore; I'm a grown, successful, and kick ass woman.

And I'm going to prove that to Scarlett, the boys, and myself, right now.

The room changes back to the lavish private lounge. I look down at my tight white dress and sexy beige heels, then over at Scarlett in her dazzling red number. Two hot powerful chicks, is who we are.

I can feel wrinkles crease my eyes as I squint at her, as if giving her some sort of telepathic instruction to assist in continuing the fight.

She nods with an understanding tilt of her head.

Wow, is she a mind reader? That would explain a lot. Like the time I found out Lola Abernathy was sexting Josh. We ran into that slut at Low Bar. A thought passed through my head of splashing my drink in her face, then I looked at Scarlett and a second later, boom! Scarlett's drink was all over that fake-boobed hussy. It was awesome. Especially because she never had a chance with Josh in the first place. He has strict one-woman vagina-vision—it's all he can think about and doesn't see anything else around him. But it was funny to see Lola look like she was melting from all that make-up running down her face. Ah, Scarlett is such a great friend.

My cheeks begin to feel strained while recalling that happy memory, from the undoubtedly huge smile on my face.

I raise my glass to Scarlett. "A toast to man versus giant ball of wood, let's see who will win."

We "cheers" and turn our focus towards the flat screen.

Chapter Eight

The Escape

Above the calm and relaxing lounge, the men get ready to release the makeshift wrecking ball.

"Okay, on the count of three, we throw it up and out with force, so it will hopefully hit the window and break on impact", the strong-minded Roman stallion, Matteo, instructs.

Everyone nods in understanding. Matteo, Josh, Rob, Liam, and Sebastian hold the structure, made from designer chair parts, above their heads.

"Three, two, one!"

They release the wooden mass with as much strength as they possibly can.

From the momentum, the five men trip forwards. After regaining their balance, they join the rest, running quickly to the ledge to watch the structure follow through.

They hear a smash.

***

"Holy shit, they cracked the glass!" I shout around the nail of my thumb that I've been biting down on while watching the boys at work.

Every time I catch myself with my fingers in my mouth, I can't help but think of my mother's nagging voice, *Alexandria, where are your manners? Stop gnawing! It's not lady-like. Our family is in the public eye and we don't want people thinking one of our daughters is a crack addict.* Pfft. She can be a real nut, sometimes.

"Meh." Scarlett shrugs. "The glass is cracked, big deal. They aren't getting in here."

She gets up and walks towards the floor-to-ceiling windows. She presses her face to the glass. "Something is shining through the wood. Dammit!"

"What? What is it?"

Paranoia strikes—I glance around the room and widen my walk, as much as I possibly can in this dress, while I hustle towards the objects sparkling in the moonlight.

She huffs then sinks her stance. With her head down and her finger pointed towards the glow, she reveals in a very sad-puppy voice,

"They attached the corkscrew, bottle opener, and couch pins to this piece of junk."

I look at her with my confused face; scrunching my forehead, creating lines I really hope do not permanently crease my skin.

She lifts her hands in the air, then brings them down quickly to hit the sides of her body. Then she sulks. "I was looking forward to them using some of those tools in the death fight."

I try to console her by patting her on the back and throwing out a joke. If I don't make light of her ridiculous behavior, who will?

"Don't worry, they will find other brutal ways to kill each other. I promise."

Even though I said it jokingly, I was telling the truth.

We turn and walk back to the cozy, white velvet, French-inspired lounge chairs. She huffs and puffs before having a self-soothing sip of red delicious.

I try to calm down with a larger-than-my-mouth-can-hold gulp of merlot. I shut my eyes, enjoying it flow down the right pipes, and hum my palate's favorite song, *Mmm mmm mmm*.

***

"I heard it break. Did it go all the way through?" Josh anxiously asks.

Tommy leans as far as he can over the ledge, sees that the glass was only cracked slightly, but decides to lie. Convincingly, too. "It's broken!"

Congratulatory high-fives and man-hugs spread around the room.

"Let's have a celebratory shot before Chad heads down," Tommy suggests.

"Good idea, lad," Henry concurs.

The men head over to the bar. Henry grabs a bottle of vodka, pours shots for everyone, and shouts, "Cheers". The same word echoes out of every guy's mouth. The shot is taken and reality sets in for Chad.

"Alright, it is time. Let's secure your harness, Chad," Tommy announces. He is fidgeting constantly, something Matteo notices, but doesn't react to.

Everyone gets up and walks over to the ledge. Matteo pulls on Chad's harness to test durability.

"Okay, when you get over this ledge, you need to hold on as tight as you can to the drainage pipe with your hands and legs. We will suspend some ropes in between the pipe and the window. When you get low enough, grab the first rope and wrap it around one of your hands and one of your feet, then swing over and wrap the other ones around the second rope, then onto the window ledge and walk into the room. Remember, you have a harness strapped onto you and we will be here for you the whole time."

Chad shakes his head to try and get out some nerves. The guys give him a pat on the back and everyone becomes silent.

Chad climbs up onto the ledge near the drainpipe, turns backwards, and lowers himself to latch onto the pipe as tight as he can.

Two shots fire and blood spatters over the ledge.

Number 1, Chad, is dead.

His body falls backwards as his face looks up at the men. The rope breaks, as the force of his body is too much to hold. He is too far down for them to see him anymore.

Chad is gone.

The men's survival instincts kick in as they all run to the centre of the room, where they now huddle scared to death.

Chapter Nine

Rock-A-Bye-Bye

"Aw, poor Chad," I say not so remorsefully. Well, I warned there would be snipers. The theory of men not being the best listeners has officially been proven.

Scarlett throws her hands in the air. "Well, it's about time someone dies! Chad was a good kid. The Mohawk didn't really fit his personality but he still looked great. It's the eyes. Green is a hard color to find these days. I would have procreated with him just for the chance that my children would have green eyes."

Did she really just say a Mohawk didn't fit his persona? He was in an Indie-rock band and had the body of Mick Jagger. He totally rocked that hair cut.

"That is the dumbest thing I've ever heard. Can you stop rambling for five seconds? This is a major turn of events. Chad is the guy that took my virginity, so it's surprising that I'm able to let him go first. Usually, girls hold on to the guy who deflowered their cherry blossom like they won't be allowed in Heaven if they let him go."

Scarlett kicks her feet up and crosses her hands behind her head. "Well, we can forget about Heaven. I think Hell is under-rated, anyways. Who wouldn't want to be somewhere permanently hot? It's like retirement, but with all of the interesting people from history."

My neck muscles loosen and my head falls backwards. Staring up at the ceiling, I notice all of the small details it has. I guess that's like everything in life—you don't see if you don't look. But in this case, I don't need to see Hell to know I don't want to ever go there. Plus, I like to ski.

"Oh, I completely disagree with you. I may have done some shady shit in this life, but I have decided to be reincarnated."

Scarlett tilts her head, as if to say, *go on.*

I copy her in kicking up my feet and cross my hands behind my head. What? She looks really comfortable. I continue, matter-of-factly. "I'm staying right here. I feel like living life as different people each time would be way more fun than sitting on some lava beach with Frank Sinatra."

Scarlett shrugs. "So where do you think Chad went?"

I take a moment to remember Chad in my head. I first met him when we were teenagers when my family and I were in Australia for a Formula One race. His father was hired as an F1 mechanical engineer and he ended up traveling around with his dad for two summers. We had supercharged sexual chemistry for each other, like regular teenagers, but were always just friends. I was a year older than him and convinced that I was too mature to date a younger guy. I still stand by that notion. But of course there are some exceptions.

It only took one summer until I gave in to his legitimate boyish charms. Some say I robbed his cradle. To most people's surprise, that made me feel pretty proud, not embarrassed, so I didn't mind.

He had the biggest crush on me but was intimidated because I was older, the daughter of a famous racecar driver, and had great, perky boobs. We spent countless days sneaking into the garage to hang out with the cars, flirt, and laugh. The weekend of my eighteenth birthday, my parents surprised me by flying Chad in for my party even though it was the off-season. We left early; he took me to my empty home and very nervously, ripped my clothes off. We kept the friendship and extreme flirting going for over a year but were never intimate again. The sexual tension eventually died out but warm feelings and good memories still remain.

With a smile on my face and feeling a little lighter, I realize that I have now let Chad go. I grab my glass of victory juice.

Why haven't I done this before? This is a great feeling! I could jump up and down right now. Though, I'm far too comfortable with my feet kicked up and wine in hand. Maybe another time.

I turn to Scarlett and answer her question. "I think Chad is in Heaven."

***

I rewind the scene in my mind to the men frantically running to the middle of the room, some tripping along the way, but all feeling one emotion more than any other. Fear. And they should, because I'm in the mood to shed a little more weight off my shoulders.

Sebastian speaks first while still trying to catch his breath. "Holy shit, she wasn't lying."

Josh holds his hands over his head. "Shit, shit, shit, shit, shit!"

Rob tries to hold back tears but is unable to. While crying and terrified, he says, "I saw into his soul as he was falling."

Liam and Clint sit in complete shock on the floor.

Henry turns his head away from the crowd and sheds a few tears.

Matteo sees Henry's soft side through his rough *Pete Doherty* exterior and decides to speak up. "Do you know what I saw? I saw the window and it wasn't broken." He stands up and with a stern voice, preaches. "We let a good man put faith and trust in us and we failed him. He died because men are vicious animals who, at the end of the day, will eat their brother to become pack leader. We should be ashamed of ourselves. But it is Tommy who deceived us all." He points at Tommy. "*His* deception led to Chad's death."

As Matteo continues to accuse, Rob walks over to the bar with his head down in shame. The responsibility of Chad's death weighs heavily on his chest and he needs to drown that pain. After almost seven years of sobriety, Rob takes the already opened bottle of vodka and drinks it like it's water. He smashes the bottle over the counter as he finishes and shouts, "Wooohooo!"

Focusing solely on Matteo's accusations, Tommy stands up to defend himself while increasing the level of his voice as he does so. "What the fuck? If anyone is responsible for Chad dying, it is Alexandria! How are you blind sons of bitches not able to see that? My number one priority is getting out of here. So ya, I lied about the window, but how does that matter? Chad was weak. He let us convince him to climb over the fucking edge even though she told us we would get sniped if we tried to escape."

The insta-drunk Rob shouts from across the room. "Don't be a dick to the dead, dude. Not cool."

Tommy forms fists beside his wide-spread legs and sticks his neck out. "Shut-up, Rob. You are just as weak as he was. It's only because you are Matteo's new pet that it wasn't you over that ledge."

Matteo puffs his chest and shakes his head as if to warn him not to say another word.

While still on the ground, Liam intervenes. "Tommy, are you looking to get a fist in your face?" He hops up with ease and leans his body forward while addressing every man. "If any of you think you didn't take part in what just happened, then you're all delusional."

Henry holds up his long arms and spreads out each finger. "Don't say there's blood on my hands when there ain't."

Unaware that Henry was not meaning to be literal, Alec looks down at his own hands. He lifts them up in the air. "Mine, either." He brings them back down and inspects them closer.

Clint watches Henry and Alec's waving arms but cannot hear them. He is still in complete shock. Even though he is the oldest of the men, he has never lost a loved one, let alone witnessed someone fall to their death. He looks over at Liam, who is sitting on the ground beside him, and sees blood on Liam's face and collar. He wipes his own face with the back of his hand and peeks with squinted eyes.

No blood. A sigh of relief escapes his chest.

He looks down at his shirt and sees spots of Chad's blood. As he inhales, anxiety floods his thoughts. All he can hear is the beating of his heart. He slowly gets up to his feet and walks over to the bar. He moves past Rob and shuffles through the bar-fridge, where he finds a can of soda and tries to get the blood spatter off his five-thousand-dollar, custom-made suit. He takes off his jacket and shirt to reveal a scar down his chest from the heart transplant surgery he had when he was eleven. The paleness of his skin speaks volumes for his workaholic nature and creates a strong contrast to the blood he is starting to scrub out. Tears do not fall from his face. All he is focused on is getting Chad off his clothes.

Josh continues to hold his hand over his head as he restlessly paces back and forth from one end of the rooftop to the other. He stops for a moment while in the middle of the room, releases his hands, and lifts his face up to the sky. He watches a few birds fly by and thinks about freedom. He imagines Chad's face as he was falling and thinks about how freeing it must have felt to know that everything was about to be over. All of the pain this world caused would disappear.

Josh blinks and for one moment, wishes it was him who went over the ledge because if he did, he wouldn't have to feel the hurt inside of his chest anymore. His thoughts are interrupted by the testosterone cloud forming over 7 and 9.

Tommy continues to red-zone at Matteo. "You son of a bitch! I am not being blamed for his death! I will fuck you up if you say another word about it!"

Matteo walks up to Tommy and sternly replies, "I don't trust you. You are a snake of a man. Shame is one hell of a heavy thing to carry around, and now you have to for the rest of your life. You are a disgrace."

Tommy clenches his fists and jaw. He sees red. He throws his right hand towards the left of Matteo's face.

Matteo's heightened awareness of movement due to the amount of time he spends hunting allows him to react quickly to Tommy's sloppy right hook. He grabs Tommy's right hand in mid-air and with only enough force to make a point, he shoves Tommy's fist in the direction it came from.

Caught off guard, Tommy stumbles backwards, loses his balance, and falls onto his ass.

He gets up quickly and rushes towards Matteo.

Deciding to intervene, Sebastian runs to Tommy and grabs him, pinning his arms to his side.

Tommy flails around to try and get out of Sebastian's grip. Frustrated with his inability to be released from the gorilla-like arms, he shouts at Matteo. "I'm going to fucking kill you!"

Liam jumps in. "Hey! Hey! Everybody calm down!"

Matteo calmly nods. "It's fine, Sebastian. Let the little monster go."

Sebastian complies. "Fine, but he is a lively one!" Then he shouts, "Aoooo aoooo!" into the air like a wolf.

Tommy charges Matteo and tries to tackle him to the ground. Matteo does not budge. Instead, he pushes Tommy off him down to the floor and steps on his hand as a warning.

Tommy gets up and delivers a punch to Matteo's gut.

From behind the crowd, Rob runs towards Tommy with the vodka bottle he had just broken in his hand.

Blind with rage, Tommy doesn't notice the surfer storming to his mentor's defense.

Rob shouts to Tommy, "Get your hands off him!"

Matteo retaliates with a strong right jab to Tommy's nose.

Disoriented, Tommy starts to see everything around him in slow motion. One second seems like one hour.

Tommy glimpses Clint topless at the bar, scrubbing his shirt, and wonders what he could be doing and realizes how similar he looks to a young version of the actor Robert Redford. His view of Clint is distorted though, as Liam's arms are in the air, waving a metaphorical white flag hoping for either party to surrender.

The next second, he finds Alec and Henry gathering near him in hopes to see a fight. He smiles as he imagines himself being friends with Henry outside of this rooftop of doom—barbequing and drinking beers with him on a workless Wednesday afternoon before heading to his shift at the bar.

Tommy stares at Alec and wonders why he has such a blank look on his face all the time, then thinks about how many hot chicks he bangs on a regular basis and envy overpowers his curiosity. Behind Alec, he notices Josh, whose eyes are pursed shut as if he is about to witness something awful.

On the third second, Tommy regains his focus and gives Matteo a death stare, but Matteo is gazing past him, with a look of pride on his face.

Tommy turns around and catches a split-second glimpse of Rob a step away with his arm raised high.

As Rob takes his last step, he jumps in the air and thrusts the broken shards of the empty vodka bottle into Tommy's neck, feeling the vibrations of each bursting vein and artery as he penetrates deeper and deeper. Rob's right arm shakes with power. Maintaining a sociopathic glare into the eyes of the frightened victim, he pulls the broken bottle out of Tommy's neck with purpose. To kill.

Rob, filled with adrenaline yet aware of the primitive deed, feels complete and utter satisfaction.

Tommy grabs his own neck with both hands as blood starts to uncontrollably gush out.

The men step back to avoid the splatter.

Tommy looks at Liam and tries to speak but is unable to. He falls to his knees then down to his side, curling his body into a fetal position.

Liam and Henry hurry to help Tommy, shoving their hands into the wound to try and stop the bleeding.

Tommy's eyes widen as his life starts to slip away. He notices the men covered in red trying to help him. He opens his mouth to speak and coughs out blood as he tries to use his vocal cords. He stops trying, lays his face sideways on the cold concrete floor, and watches his own blood pool around his face.

Number 9, Tommy, is dead.

Chapter Ten

Hate Male

Scarlett and I find ourselves standing inches away from the television screen. The intensity of what we just watched fills us with what feels like a lifetime supply of adrenaline.

I have not blinked since the bottle entered his neck. My mouth is dropped open and my heart beats so fast that I start to sweat. This one, I did not initially see coming. I mean, from the time I've known Rob, I always knew him to be a loyal and caring guy. But the first of the group to kill, that's a surprise! A part of me feels proud and the other side is relieved I wasn't around long enough to see his switch get flipped like that. I suppose I should be sad for Tommy, but the tingling in my body from shock is overpowering my thought process.

Meaning to be comforting, Scarlett grabs my hand and clenches it with all her might. I hold on tighter.

The muscles in my arm start to feel numb. I shake it a few times and let her hand go.

With my eyes still wide open, I turn my head away from the screen to look at Scarlett.

Our faces, accidentally, get so close our noses touch.

Ignoring the awkward proximity, I take a deep breath. "Wine?"

She nods. "Wine."

She grabs the vintage bottle and heads back to the lounge chairs to refill our glasses.

My feet are firmly planted in front of the screen and my stare is locked on the men as they come to terms with the wicked recent event.

Scarlett fills the glasses to the rim, sips both so they don't spill, and carries them over to me. I stop her mid-way across the room. "Let's sit."

She nods again. "Let's sit."

My hand shakes as I let the luscious liquid pour into my mouth through my pursed lips, until the glass is half empty. I shut my eyes, take a deep breath, and feel my heartbeat start to slow down. It's about time. Sweating does absolutely nothing good for me. I get all red and patchy, then my upper lip forms a liquid mustache—not exactly the most attractive look.

I scrunch my nose and can feel the frown lines crease my forehead to the maximum. Now that my pulse is regular, I have room for thought. They immediately turn negative. Tommy is so stupid. What a mess of a man. Can't he ever just act like an adult for ten minutes? I never should have let him in, he's like a tick—I don't want him under my skin, but he buried himself in there somehow and now it's increasingly difficult to get him out. My jaw muscles start to clench and so does my fist as I gesture to the flat screen.

"Tommy's inability to act maturely or rationally in any situation was the root cause of his demise. He did this to himself."

After anxiously waiting for me to speak first, Scarlett blurts out. "Well, that was disgusting." She makes a repulsed face then shrugs. "But necessary. Goodbye, Number 9."

I smoothen my forehead with the back of my hand to encourage my mind, and skin, to let go of the anger. I would use both hands but the magnificent French vintage is more important. I look over at her and nod in agreement.

She continues. "Tommy was a god-awful mess of a man."

Ha. That's exactly what I just thought. At least I'm not alone on that one. And it's so true. He's like a kid, and there is no point in getting mad at the actions of an infant. Children will be children. I'm just glad he's not mine. The tension in my jaw releases. I concur. "Ya, he needed to go. He was disrupting the flow with his wild-card tantrums."

Scarlett turns her chair slightly to face me, crosses her legs, places her elbow on her knee and hand on her chin—the thinking woman pose—and asks the question.

"Why do you still have attachments to him? You never really liked him that much to begin with, and we all assumed he was like a side project to keep you entertained during a slow few months at work."

I wonder who she means by *we all*. Who was talking about me, saying that I was so cold hearted to simply play with a guy while sales were low? I laugh. Okay, maybe there is some truth to that. What can I say? Projects are fun. Does that make me an awful person? Oh shit, it does. Well, maybe I will be joining Scar and Sinatra in the scorching sun, after all.

"To be honest, he was like a wounded bird that I found and desperately wanted to slap in the face and tell it to get its shit together and start acting like a grown bird."

Okay, the bird analogy is not my best.

"I thought I let him go a long time ago but I think I was holding on to some anger."

Maintaining her thinking pose, Scarlett investigates. "Anger? For what? The break-up was mutual."

When Tommy and I broke up, we promised to still be friends because without each other in our lives, it wouldn't be the same. We never saw or spoke to each other after that day.

Shutting my eyes tight, a little shame invades me. "I think I gave up on him because I realized I wasn't enough. He was in love with someone in his past and I couldn't be enough for him to get over that."

Throwing her hands up in the air, Scarlett huffs. "Oh please, he was a lost cause and you knew it!"

Noticing I was not replying, she continues with her head held high. "And tonight, you channeled your anger and he died by his own poison puncturing his carotid artery. Very poetic, if I do say so myself."

Scar always knows how to make me smile. And she was right—it was really fun to have an empty liquor bottle being his way out. Lord knows he had enough of those lying around his house. Tommy definitely had a problem, and this was one hell of a way to point that out.

"It was quite satisfying. I always knew he wasn't the one for me. I mean, he was an alcoholic Vegas bartender without any ambition. Actually, correction, he did have a dream—to one day fight Mike Tyson and win. Which might as well be a death wish considering his lack of coordination, height, weight, fighting skill and, well, ability to be sober for any period of time."

Scarlett chuckles and shakes her head like a disappointed parent.

I hate to admit it, but it was definitely my ego holding on to this one. I won't let Scar know that, though. It would give her too much pleasure, and I'm not ready for her *I told ya so* dance just yet.

"Taking a step back and just letting these events unfold as they would, allowed my mind to think a little clearer, and see him for his true self—someone not worth being attached to."

She picks up her glass and shuts her eyes as she tastes pure excellence. "It's not your fault, Alex. The truth is hard to see behind a handsome face. Mother God knows I've dated some monsters who at first looked like Zac Efron, but sooner or later show their Gary Busey-like mug-shot."

I can feel my long eyelashes graze my brow as my eyes widen. "Zac Efron, really?" I try and hide a giggle with my Merlot. I'm only teasing her—I think he's sexy, too.

She places her glass down with care, then immediately flails her hands around in the air—the true sign of her Italian heritage. "That's what you chose to hear? I just said Tommy is a soon-to-be arrested crazy man!"

I stare at the screen, ignoring Scar for a moment. Having an ego is a hell of a thing. To think that all this time, I've been holding onto someone I don't even really like as a human being, all because I have a need to win. Win what? Who knows, but Tommy is one I'm glad I didn't.

I turn to Scarlett, who I notice, has moved on to checking her cuticles. "I feel a lot better now."

She puts her hand on my shoulder and pets it. "Good. So the other deaths won't be so gruesome?"

A mischievous smile curls up my cheeks. "Oh, we've just started."

***

The room is so silent and still that it looks as if someone pressed a pause button.

Rob drops the murder weapon onto the concrete. The smashing of the glass resounds through everyone's ears like a siren. The noise continues to sound in Rob's head. He jerks his hands up to his ears, trying to shut out the echo of what he just did.

Liam and Henry stay kneeling next to Tommy's lifeless body. Henry looks down at his hands and sees more blood than he has ever seen before.

Alec holds his hand over his mouth and mumbles, "I think I'm gonna puke." He runs over to the back corner of the building and projectile vomits.

Josh finally opens his eyes. The last thing he saw was Rob's arm in the air and now he sees a life drained all over the floor. He's relieved that it is Tommy and not him. He takes a heavy inhale and fills his body with a new appetite for life. A devilish smile cracks the side of his mouth. He is now determined to be the last man standing.

Sebastian is humming to himself while walking backwards, one step at a time. This was the coping mechanism he used as a child when his parents were fighting near him. He'd hum to drown out the noise, step back to avoid additional confrontation, and keep his eyes open so he could calculate the intensity level. If it was above a four, he would run to the phone and call the police. His father went to prison when he was eleven and has not yet been released.

Hovering above Tommy, Matteo realizes the result of his mentorship to Rob and can't help but feel responsible for creating this demon. He walks up to Rob, puts his arm around him, and directs him towards the bar.

Rob flinches, opens his eyes, and sees Matteo. "Sorry if I've disappointed you."

Matteo responds like a father would. "You could never disappoint me. Let's clean you up and discuss the repercussions of your actions."

Matteo's natural instincts set in as he starts mentally structuring a strategy for survival. He realizes that most men are alone and his chances of winning will increase if he teams up with someone to use as a pawn. He looks over at the vulnerable Rob. "We are in this together now."

As the two head towards the bar, Clint snaps back to reality and notices everyone quickly moving on from the horrific murder that just took place. Still topless and safely behind the bar, he shouts so everyone can hear. "We have to do something about the dead body in the middle of the room!"

Everyone stops and looks over at him.

Sebastian shouts back sarcastically, "You're still here?"

Clint mumbles to himself. "Not by will."

Chapter Eleven

Team Up or Die

As time passes, the sky's darkness deepens. The men are only visible by the radiance of the moon and in-ground lights of the rooftop lounge.

Standing over one of the recessed floor spotlights with his hands on his hips, Sebastian glows like Superman on display. The rest of the men avoid the pockets of luminescence in the floor to not alter their already acclimatized night vision.

Alec, Henry, and Liam are near the ledge trying to get Alec's lighter to work. Henry shakes it, flicks the igniter over and over, but still only sees sparks.

With a joint hanging from his mouth and the look of impatience on his face, Alec grabs the lighter back from Henry, turns his back to the wind, covers his face, and lights up.

Liam and Henry watch the exhaled smoke rise above Alec's head and feel the yearning for that calming agent to enter their lungs as well. Alec turns around, passes the joint to Henry, and closes his eyes with the hope that he is able, for just this moment at least, to escape reality.

On his way back from cleaning his shirt and putting it back on, Clint passes Sebastian. "Let's go sit with Josh. He knows Alexandria the most and may have an idea of how to get us out of here alive. He is our best bet right now."

Disappointed with having to move from his spotlight, Sebastian shakes his head. "Wait, let me put my game face on first." He pauses for two seconds. "Okay, I'm ready now. Let's go."

Clint rolls his eyes, gives Sebastian a single pat to the back, and heads towards Josh.

Sitting in one of the only three assembled leather chairs left, Josh watches Sebastian and Clint compete in the non-existent *Who Has The Better Swagger* competition. He thinks in his head, *what did Alexandria ever see in these guys? Sure they are both tall, make a lot of money, and have curiously perfect hair, but Sebastian is strange, douchey, and looks like an Albino Gorilla. When did that become her type? And Clint is a goddamn lawyer. She hates lawyers. I am way better than them.*

Keeping his thoughts to himself, he greets the boys with a cool-guy head nod. "Hey, what's up? Take a seat."

Sebastian and Clint pull the last two chairs close to Josh, creating a triangle of chiseled features.

"Hey, Josh," Sebastian starts. "Clint has an interesting proposition for the three of us."

"Oh ya, what's that? You think we should kill Alec? Me, too," Josh says too quickly for them to understand.

Clint ignores Josh's mumble. "I think the three of us should team up. Sebastian is the strongest of the group, I have the best negotiating skills, and you have the most fervor."

Sebastian nods. "Since you know Alexandria the most, we're hoping that you may know something we don't. Something that could save our lives, or at the very least, get us to the last three."

Josh proudly responds, "I do know her the best." He thinks for a second. "She may have left clues to survival around here, and possibly weapons."

Clint anxiously questions, "Weapons? You think she hid weapons?"

Sebastian nods again. "That wouldn't surprise me. She was always into some freaky shit in bed."

Josh immediately scowls but thinks it's in his best interest to contain his Hyde for now and kill Sebastian later.

Clint looks over at another group gathering. He first thinks they are also talking strategy, until he sees Liam pass something to Alec and exhale smoke. "Are they smoking pot over there?" he judgingly asks Josh and Sebastian.

Sebastian props his hands on the arms to lift himself out of the plush leather chair. "I could use some of that right now."

"Sit down," Clint demands. "This is good for us. Let them get high. We will have the upper hand over the three of them now."

Sebastian sits back down. "So our only worry now is psycho surfer Rob and his master, Wise Man MacGyver Matteo."

After giving Sebastian a courtesy chuckle, Josh proposes, "Instead of worrying about them, why don't we join forces, for now, of course, and get rid of the three stoners together?"

Agreeing but still wanting to be the leader of the plan, Clint speculates, "That might just work. Rob is vulnerable right now because people are afraid of him. Matteo is in an unfortunate position because he is tied to Rob whether he likes it or not. No one is talking to them. If we can discretely get them on board, Liam, Alec, and Henry will have no idea what hit them."

Sebastian nods. "I agree. I would like to make it clear though, that Matteo and Rob are not to be trusted. Bringing them in on this will only be to get them off our backs. As soon as we are done with them, they need to go. The three of us need to stick together. Agreed?"

Josh and Clint simultaneously state, "Agreed."

Clint delegates. "Okay, Josh, you go look for weapons in places you think Alexandria may have hid them, but do not get noticed. If you find anything, leave it where it is then come back to tell us. Having weapons out in the open will create one massive fight and that is not what we want. We want strategy."

Josh nods.

Standing with his hands on his hips and legs spread wide—his power stance—Clint continues. "Sebastian and I will go talk to Matteo and Rob at the bar. If they are on board, we will give you a thumbs-up."

Sebastian interrupts. "And if they don't, I will howl twice into the air. That will signal you to bring the weapons over so we can kill them first."

Clint immediately puts his hand up. "No, bad idea. If you howl, you'll get a broken bottle in your neck like poor Tommy." He shakes his head. "If they don't agree, we will reconvene and come up with another plan."

Josh twists his curls with his fingers. "I actually agree with Sebastian. If they disagree, they may go over to the other boys and tell them what we planned." He stops as he sees Clint notice his nervous habit. He puts his hand back down to his side and continues. "Then we are the ones shit out of luck."

"Okay, fuck, okay." Clint rubs his temples to get his thoughts together. "So our plan B is to kill Rob and Matteo. If the other boys ask why, we will tell them it was to avenge Tommy's death." He starts to walk over but notices his partner does not follow. "Sebastian, let's do this before their high wears off."

Two whisky-on-the-rocks deep, Matteo entertains Rob with life lessons from great wise men as Rob washes blood off himself and his clothes.

"Washing blood off your clothes is like cleansing the sins that blood holds. Every man sins, but it is those who do not forgive themselves for being human that are the real sinners. You should not feel any guilt for what you did, Rob. You are a brave man and I respect that." Matteo finishes his second whisky and realizes he does not feel tipsy. He is proud of his tolerance level.

He notices Rob's head hanging particularly low, realizes that his words of wisdom were not helping. In order for him to rely on Rob for help in this fight, he needs him to get back to normal. "Rob, I heard you were the only one of all the men that left Alexandria and not the other way around. Why?"

Rob raises his head and shirt. He lifts the garment high enough for the moon's light to show the red stains covering almost the entire surface. He throws the fabric down. "This shirt is fucked, good thing it's summer." He addresses Matteo's question with a bit more pep in his voice. "Actually, I didn't leave her. My sponsor did."

Matteo stops Rob from continuing. "The blonds are heading over here. Continue to act upset. We don't want them to know we are actually satisfied with the recent death."

Rob tries to say something, 'But I— "

"Shh." Matteo stops him and holds his hand up, gesturing for Rob to obey.

"Hey, boys." Matteo fakes a smile as Sebastian and Clint approach them.

Rob fumbles as he grabs glasses for his guests. "Can I get you a drink? I once worked as a bartender in Tahiti and didn't wear a shirt then, either." His typical surfer chuckle follows.

Sebastian purposely avoids eye contact and looks at the impressive selection of imports. "Ya, sure. Thanks, bud. I'll have a Jägermeister." Pronouncing it in a perfect German accent.

Clint glances at the bottle of Gran Patrón Platinum, but shakes his head. "No, I'm good, thanks." He takes a seat beside Matteo. "Well, we came over here to see how you were doing, Rob, but it seems like you're doing just fine."

Matteo stands up and leans over the bar to pat Rob, who is too far away, so he grabs a bottle of bar lime instead. "No, he is just putting on a happy face for you guys, isn't that right, Rob? You have been depressed and upset since the incident, right?"

"Oh, ya, I'm super bummed, but he was trying to kill my boy and I couldn't let that happen." He puts his hands in the air. "I plead self-defense." Another surfer chuckle follows.

Slightly regretting his decision to join teams, but acting chummy so he can get in good with Rob, Clint forces out a chuckle as well.

Rob puts Sebastian's drink down on the counter and Sebastian decides to get straight to the point. "Listen, boys. Josh, Clint, and I want to make an alliance with you two. The three other guys are getting high in the corner and we think it is a good idea to take them out while they are disoriented."

Matteo looks over at the boys near the ledge. He gets upset that he didn't notice what they were doing and come up with this plan himself. He reaches his hand out towards Clint, palm facing upwards. In less than a second, a strong shake ensues. "We're in."

Chapter Twelve

I'll Show You Mine

Scarlett holds her hand up in the air and mimics, "Obey me, I am Matteo, protector of weak men and slayer of wild beasts that roam the forest."

I jump out of the chair in my tight white dress and pretend to hold a sword and shield. "I will protect you, young surfer, but only if you do as I say, and not as I do."

We burst out laughing. It seems the luscious liquid disappearing from these bottles may have an effect on us. But I'm having a fab time, so the more the merrier is my new motto.

Scarlett gestures with her foot for me to sit down. "After the craziness that just happened, you would think I'd be happy with some deal-making side plots, but really, I just want someone else to die. Now!"

Sitting back down, I grab my glass of red delicious and try not to spill it as I cross my legs. "I have to admit I am getting anxious, too." I can feel my fingers twisting the bottom corner of my lip again. "Do you think Liam would catch on to what the others planned?"

Scarlett slaps my hand away from my mouth. "Stop doing that, it looks weird and there is no reason to be nervous." She shakes her head and takes another sip, staring at me the whole time.

"About Liam, All I have to say is, dude's got a black belt and I am really looking forward to him using it." She stands up and walks over to the flat screen, where she points at Josh as he rummages through the still upholstered leather lounge chairs. "You didn't really hide weapons up there, did you?"

I smile at her innocently, tilting my head and flickering my eyelashes. If anyone should know I'm not as innocent as I look, it's her. "Umm, yap."

"Whaatt!" She raises her voice about eight octaves higher than regular. "I was up there in this room full of weapons and clearly sadistic men? Here I thought the corkscrew was the deadliest thing in this room. Cock sucker, Alexandria! That is some shit!"

I laugh and shake my head. She is so dramatic, and so loud. She should come with a warning like our music players: level thirteen or higher indicates that it *may harm your hearing if you listen for too long*. Her voice is more like a twenty. Maybe I can bring earmuffs back in style through my shop. Worth a try.

I reach my hand out to cover her mouth. "You were never going to get hurt, dummy. They didn't know they were there to fight to the death yet. I figured if they found anything, they would probably question it, but not use it."

"Comforting." She crosses her arms and huffs.

I lift her lowered head up not so gently. "You do realize everything is in my control, right? Why would I have something happen to you? What a stupid comment." I wave my hand in the air. "Moving on."

Scarlett goes through her emotions until she hits acceptance. "Huh. Right. But this control thing is not healthy." She copies my wave. "Okay. Moving on."

She distracts herself by trying to reach the hanging chandelier, which prompts a switch in her train of thought. "I like the touch that Alec is packing dubes in his jacket. Hilarious. Was he really that big of a pothead? He is a professional athlete, for God sakes."

I shake my head in disapproval. "Yep. He never really made any smart choices off the field."

Thoughts of waking up beside him with a joint in his mouth make me frown. But being in bed with him, even if it was a little smoky, made smile, then admit, "But he was a phenomenal lover. Ugh, just thinking about his perfectly sculpted butt sends shivers down my body into my vaginal canal. Sometimes, I think if he would have been mute, and faithful, we would have had the perfect relationship—except he was a religious southern American boy, a Republican, he used to eat pot brownies for breakfast, and he didn't take his career seriously. We had absolutely nothing in common. So I guess just the sex is what I'm holding on to."

"Completely understandable." Scarlett nods. "I once went back to a guy who stole from me because he was that good in bed."

"What?" I laugh. "That's insane."

She shrugs as she takes a sip of liquid lust. "Mind-blowing sex is hard to find."

She's kidding herself if she thinks she can jump off this topic so fast. I ask, "Did he steal from you the second time?"

Her face scrunches. "Kind of. I let him live with me rent-free for six months. He also never bought a single grocery, that cheap ass."

While walking back to the lounge chairs, I catch myself tilting my head side to side with confusion. So, let me get this straight—she got robbed after a phenomenal romp, then harbored the criminal for half a year. That's what I just heard, right? It's official; my best friend is a crazy person. "I'm not even going to entertain this any longer because it is that ludicrous."

She follows me back, sits down, and crosses her legs, facing me. "Is it? Really?" She takes another sip of Merlot. "Is it more ludicrous than Sebastian wanting to wear your underwear on his face during sex?"

I turn my head to think for a moment. "Yes," I blurt out not so convincingly.

Scarlett takes another thirty dollar gulp of the rare vintage.

I reach my hand out, gesturing for her to slow down. "Not so fast, lush. You want to remember this in the morning, right?"

She sticks her bottom lip out and pouts. "Well, *they* are drinking!"

I lean closer to her and lift my arm up, pointing to the rooftop. "Ya, but they are about to die!"

I don't even know why I'm judging. We're killing my exes here; this is not the last bottle of Nature's healing juice we'll be finishing tonight. That's for certain.

She jitters in her seat. "Oh good! Which one? Who dies next?"

I bring my arm down and lean as far back as possible in the chair. After crossing my legs, I place my hands softly on my knee. I'm going to need to get comfortable for this one. I lock my eyes on the screen and divulge, "Not one, three."

Chapter Thirteen

Playing Nice

Clint gestures a thumbs-up across the room to Josh as he watches him search underneath the ledge for a taped-up weapon.

Josh not so discretely waves his hand in the air.

Clint turns his back and faces the bar, trying not to draw attention to the newly joined teammates.

Matteo blurts out the side of his mouth, "What is Josh doing?"

"He is, um, taking a piss," Sebastian lies as he finishes his shot of Jäger.

"Oh, right, I'll do that, too." Matteo stares at his partner. "Rob, you good?"

Matteo gets off the stool and heads towards an empty corner.

Rob understands the command and moves out from behind the bar to follow him.

Sebastian hops behind the bar to assume the role. He pours two shots and hands one to Clint. "I don't think they suspect anything."

Clint waves his hand, declining the drink. "No, I don't think they do, either. Get Josh over here before their washroom break is over. We need to know if he found anything."

Sebastian pops his head up. "Can I howl?"

"No. Just look at him and gesture to come back. I've already called enough attention to us."

Sebastian gets Josh's attention by clinking together two glasses.

Clint rolls his eyes but is happy to see no one noticed.

Within seconds, Josh arrives at the bar.

A whole minute passes without words. Sebastian breaks the silence and bluntly asks, "So? What have you found?"

"Oh. Ya, nothing," Josh answers untruthfully.

He thinks to himself, *if I tell them I found an arrow, then they will send me on a hunt for a bow. The longer I am out of the loop, the more likely I am to be a target. I refuse to be anyone's lap dog. Fuck them. Okay, come up with something convincing to say as to why there aren't any weapons in the open.*

Josh shares out loud, "I thought you called me back to check under the bar. Anywhere else would be too noticeable."

"Well, what are you waiting for? They will be back soon," Clint impatiently huffs.

Josh sneaks behind the bar and starts to search quietly.

Over by the new pissing corner, Matteo whispers to Rob, "What do you think about Josh and the blonds?"

Delighted to be asked his opinion, Rob responds, "I think we can trust them."

Matteo coldly shuts him down. "Wrong. We can't trust any of them." He looks over at Rob as he zips up his pants. "A fool keeps his enemies close and assumes he can conquer them. A wise man assumes his friends are his enemies so he will never be fooled."

Trying to decipher Matteo's words, Rob scratches his head and stares into space. "So we kill them?"

Matteo puts his arm around Rob as they turn and head back towards the bar. "No, young Rob. We befriend them, go with their plan, then kill them," he whispers.

Rob nods and softly agrees. "Okay, boss."

Clint taps Josh on the head. "Okay, they are heading back. Get up."

While still crouching behind the bar, Josh looks up at Clint and Sebastian. "There is an axe under here."

They would have found it so sharing this info with them binds my allegiance. Smooth. Alexandria would be impressed.

Sebastian's and Clint's eyes widen.

Josh pops up in time as Rob and Matteo arrive. "Look what I found!"

Sebastian and Clint clench their jaws together and shake their heads slightly as they widen their eyes more.

Josh sees their panic and smiles. "An 80-year-old bottle of Scotch. Let's have a taste while we plan our attack."

Everyone puts a pretend-happy face on and nods in approval.

As Josh lines up glasses for the fivesome, Liam, Alec and Henry finish the joint.

"I haven't gotten this high since yesterday," Henry jokes.

The boys laugh harder than they would sober.

Alec slides his back down the ledge wall. "I could take a serious nap right now."

Henry sits down beside him. "I'm right there with ya, lad. How long d'you suppose Alexandria will keep us here?"

Still standing and looking around the room with a heightened sense of paranoia, Liam responds, "When she realizes no one will kill anyone else. She is stubborn, so it may be a while." He looks at the men gathered at the bar and thinks to himself, *or not.*

Over at the bar, the men drink their Scotch and begin to plot an assassination.

Matteo lifts his hand in the air. "I want to hear the plan, but first I want to advise that the quicker we do this, the easier."

Sebastian nods. "I agree. What we need to do is call a mass meeting and ambush them."

Clint shakes his head. "Ambush them with what? We don't have any weapons."

Matteo waves the comment away. "Not obvious ones, but we do have a whole pile of wire from the canopy lights that we used as rope for the wood and for Chad." He closes his eyes and bows his head. "Rest his soul."

Josh furrows his brows at the righteous Roman. "Are you suggesting we strangle them?"

Matteo slowly lifts his head. "Yes."

Attempting to regain the leadership position, Clint jumps in. "Well, I don't see any better option. That is what we will do." He drops his fist down on the bar top like a gavel. "Rob, discretely grab the pile of Christmas lights. Matteo, how did you cut it last time?"

"With my pocket knife. I carry it with me wherever I go."

Feeling slightly afraid of Wise Man McGyver but acting impressed, Clint smiles at Matteo. "That's perfect." He continues to delegate. "Josh, you and Sebastian go over to the party boys and tell them we are going to have a group meeting to discuss what to do next. I will pour some drinks for everyone and make noise to distract them from Rob gathering our murder weapons."

Matteo and Rob walk over to the bundle of lights. Rob watches as Matteo slices each wire long enough to wrap around his hand but small enough to fit in each man's pocket. He wonders if Matteo has done this before, as his movements seem methodical. His thoughts are interrupted as Matteo shouts, "Hey", to get his attention. He stumbles backwards and lands on his ass.

Matteo crouches beside him and cups the side of his face. "You can do this. You are a predator, not the prey. Do not let yourself get distracted." He places the cord in Rob's hand and stares at him with eyes like a lion, void of fear. He firmly states with his jaw clenched and chest muscles puffed out, "Focus. Breathe. Kill."

Rob makes a fist around the wire, stands up and confirms, “I’m a predator.”

As Sebastian and Josh head over to the ledge, Clint starts clinking glasses and bottles while singing obnoxiously loud. "I can't get no…bum, bum, bum…satisfaction".

Liam sees Josh and Sebastian approaching and starts to ramble. “Hey boys, you just missed an intense session. I can barely open my eyes. How long do you think Alexandria is going to keep us here? I’m fuckin tired as hell. This pot is a real downer. She doesn’t actually expect us to listen to her, right? She does have a controlling side, even as a friend. She won’t be happy when she sees we refused to participate but she’ll get over it. Man, I wish she were here right now so I could talk to her. She gets these sadistic ideas every now and then but hasn’t actually followed through with them ever. This is taking it way too far. How do you think she pulled off getting snipers? Snipers are so cool. She probably went to some military camp and told them she would show them her boobs if they did this for a few hours. Hey, maybe they are gone by now? Or maybe she is sleeping with one of them as we speak, or all of them? Whoa. I think my inner stoner has been awakened. Wait. How cool would it be if we all had little men inside of us that would pop out when we were high and say inspirational stuff? Cooler than having snipers, for sure. Wait. Maybe not. Snipers are seriously cool—"

Sebastian slides his hand over Liam's mouth. "And so concludes the most useless rant in the history of man."

Alec laughs at Sebastian's comment then gets distracted by the noise at the bar. He sees Clint pouring something and is instantly reminded that he is thirsty. Pasties have set in. Standard.

Josh, however, is getting irritated with the attention span of the stoners. "So guys, we're here to ask if you'd like to come over to the bar for some drinks. If we have to wait for Ally to give in, we might as well do it with some free expensive booze in our guts."

Henry reaches his arm up for a high five. "Alright! I'm always up for a drink."

Sebastian meets his extended arm then turns and skips towards the bar.

The guys brush off his strangeness and follow. Josh takes about ten steps and arrives next to Clint, who tosses him a wink as if to say *good job.*

Henry, Alec, and Liam take a seat on the swivel stools. Alec starts to spin. Henry copies him.

They stop when Clint bellows, "Who wants a drink?"

While the mere sight of liquid distracts the seated high squad, Matteo and Rob arrive behind them at the bar. Matteo slips the measured and neatly folded cords into the back of Sebastian's and Josh's pants.

Then, like activated sleeper cells, Rob, Matteo, and Sebastian wrap the cords around their hands, and then their hands around Liam's, Henry's, and Alec's necks.

Chapter Fourteen

Letting Go

Clint, behind the bar, watches the scared look on each man's face. He gets a bad feeling about this plan. He sees Josh standing beside the bar, realizes his fight or flight mode must be turned on, and the red in his eyes means fight.

In shock, Alec starts to flail around.

Sebastian holds Alec's life in his hands and he feels stronger than ever.

Alec tries to move forward. Not helping. He pushes his head backwards and feels someone's body.

With pure hatred and jealously in his heart for Alec, Josh shouts to Sebastian, "Sebastian! This one is mine."

Sebastian looks over at Josh, opens his hands, takes a step back, and willingly lets go of Alec.

Alec feels the pressure on his neck ease and starts to cough uncontrollably.

Josh, ready with his own cord wrapped around his hands, throws his arms over Alec's head and tightens with all his might. Josh feels power. Josh feels vengeance. Josh is determined to end Alec's life.

Ignoring Alec's arms flailing around and hitting his face, he grips tighter. His own skin rips as the cord starts to cut into his hands. The pain only focuses him more. He plants his feet firmly on the ground and pulls the cord and Alec's head towards him.

The tightened cord cuts into Alec's neck and blood starts seeping out of his torn flesh. Alec's life slips away.

Josh feels Alec's body go limp but he doesn't care. He keeps holding the cord tighter and tighter as Alec's blood drip down his hands. He lets go.

Alec's head and body collapse forwards.

The adrenaline in Josh's body gives him a high he has never felt before. He feels fulfilled. He feels whole. He fantasized about killing Alec before, and now he has.

The famous American football player and my Number 3, Alec Lonza, is dead.

Beside Alec, in a panic, is Henry, with his life in Matteo's hands. Henry's immediate reaction is to kick and scream. Unable to utter a sound, he instead props his long legs against the bar and pushes himself backwards, falling to the floor. On his back, he looks up into his attacker's eyes and Matteo stares back with determination in his. Henry tries to speak. He watches Matteo lift his foot and lets out a light whisper pleading, "don't".

Rob is struggling to hold on to Liam.

Having defense and combat training from succeeding in achieving a black belt, Liam tenses the muscles in his neck. He uses one hand to try and loosen the cord from his neck, and the other arm to elbow Rob in the ribs. Liam catches a moment of luck when Rob looks over at Matteo losing hold of Henry. His distraction gives Liam a window of opportunity. Liam grabs the wire around his neck with his fingers, pulls the cord away from his neck, and jerks Rob closer towards him. He throws his head backwards, hits Rob's chest, and knocks the wind out of him.

Rob falls onto him, gasping for air. He grabs Rob's flowy surfer locks over his shoulder and wraps his muscular arm around

Rob's neck. Rob starts to squirm as he is losing control of the situation, and consciousness.

Clint watches the plan fucking up right before his eyes and he stands in front of the mess as frozen as a corpse. What feels like three hours is in fact just a few seconds. He doesn't understand why he can't move or why his body is shaking.

Matteo is standing tall and staring down at the Brit. He stomps his foot on Henry's larynx and uses every muscle in his body to force down a fatal amount of pressure. Being in control of the balance of life and death fuels him. He takes a deep breath in and out then steadies his posture, like he is preparing to shoot a wild boar. Shifting all on his weight to his right leg, he pushes down harder and crunches his prey's neck bone under his foot.

Henry's eyes widen as they fill with blood. His head falls to the side when Matteo lifts his limb off the lifeless lad's neck.

Number 2, Henry, is dead.

Noticing Rob struggling, Sebastian runs behind the bar and starts shaking the stunned Clint who is not responding. Sebastian smacks Clint across the face.

Clint comes back to reality and blinks at Sebastian. "What?"

Sebastian shouts, "Move!" and throws Clint to the ground. He grabs the axe from under the bar, raises it over his head, and aims it in front of Liam.

Liam glances forward for just a moment and sees a large object swooping towards him. He shuts his eyes tight and thinks of his mother.

The axe entering flesh makes a sound quieter than the cracking of a coconut.

Liam feels no pain. He wonders if Tommy's death was also this painless. He releases his grip of Rob and embraces the thought of dying.

Two seconds pass. Liam opens his eyes and sees blood all over his body. He hears Sebastian scream, "No!" Then he looks down at Rob's lifeless corpse.

Rob lies on the ground with the axe in the back of his head. Blood continues to pool around his body. His eyes are still open but there is no life left in them.

Number 4, surfer Rob, is dead.

Chapter Fifteen

Ruby-Colored Encouragement

Scarlett and I find ourselves sitting on the same chair, she on the arm and I in the seat, with both of our legs curled up as close as possible to our chests. My hand grasps hers so tightly I can feel it begin to numb.

Our eyes are glued to the flat-screen. There is so much blood. It is almost impossible to see anything but red.

Wow.

I think I'm in shock from what just happened. My whole body is pulsing and my heart beating so fast from the adrenaline pumping through it, like I was just stuck with a shot of epinephrine.

But it's not just me feeling this way. I press my ear against her shoulder. "Can you hear that?"

"Hear what? My veins bursting? Because that's what I assume is happening inside of me. I might pass out. If I faint, please catch me." She rests the back of her hand on her forehead and sighs.

Well, she's basically already on top of me, so at least I don't have to worry about her falling. There are more important things occupying my attention right now—like blood and guts and axes in heads! Maybe not guts, but there's definitely some brain goop. Ew. My body shivers at the thought.

Scarlett slides off the arm and right onto my lap. "That was the most intense thing I've experienced in a long time. Of course, nothing tops the time I tried peyote with an Indian tribe in Northern Mexico."

I feel a bubble in my throat and push her back up just in time for my body to instinctually jerk forwards. Oh, shit. I think I'm going to be sick. I shouldn't have thought of Rob's leaking head matter. Too disgusting for my stomach to handle. Crap. I grab my neck. I can feel liquid creep into my mouth. I toss my head back and swallow. Well, that was gross.

My insides feel something. It is a little like nausea and a lot like remorse. I wanted to find a way to let them go, but maybe my body is too used to having them there, and like an addict weaning off the hooch, I'm going through withdrawals. I feel so confused. Partly because their deaths give my mind a deep seeded satisfaction.

So why is my anatomy giving me such an opposite reaction? I think the violent approach is working, though, because when I try and imagine them now, I don't see them at our happiest moments.

I see them dead.

"That's it!" I hop out of my seat and lift my arms in the air like a fan celebrating their team scoring a point. Excitement replaces the adrenaline in my chest and I cheer, "Scarlett, they are dead to me!"

She starts laughing.

I snap my head toward her and frown. "What are you laughing at? Three guys were just brutally murdered. I'm supposed to be the sadistic one. Stop trying to steal my character trait."

Scarlett straightens her back and lifts her eyebrows, probably wondering what she said wrong.

I lift up my hand over my head and move it slowly down my face—every inch reveals more of my sneaky smile. "Gotcha!"

She lightly slaps my arm and rolls her eyes. "You jerk." She turns to the screen, laughs, then slurs, "2, 3, 4. Bing, Bang, Boom. Ha ha ha. Dead as a doornail." She sloppily jumps up, tries to bend her knees in her latex-tight red number but can't, and points to the television. "Ha ha. Rob with the axe on the rooftop! I win Clue!"

She sounds like a proper nut job, and from the back, looks like one, too. When did her hair get so messy? I watch her wobble and notice how her foot is bent to the side. How is she maintaining balance like that? I should probably go stand by her, in case she buckles over. I wave my hand. Nah, I think I'll let her handle the simple task of standing up, on her own this time. I'm beat. I crash back down in my chair. "Well, you're drunk. That makes sense. You've basically had that glass in your mouth like a baby with a pacifier all night."

Scarlett turns to face me, raises her glass then takes another sip. "Alexandria, if you think a few glasses of adult grape juice will get me drunk, you underestimate the Italian in me. We drink this stuff for breakfast."

She pauses, then stumbles and grabs the side of my lounge chair to regain balance. She lets out a very classy belch, then admits, "I think I'm gonna puke."

I can feel my face scrunching with judgment. I lift my hand up to pinch my nose closed. Gross! That burp smelled like tacos. How is that even possible? We had stir-fry for dinner.

I grab her arms with both hands and guide her over to her seat. "Oh Scarlett, you cheap drunk. Sit down. I'm not falling for your empty threats. You aren't going to puke."

She makes a very loud swallowing noise then pinches her cheeks. "Okay, I'm better now."

I brush off the fact she just swallowed her own vomit, because well, I was just in that position a few minutes ago. It happens to the best of us. And now that's out of the way, I suppose more won't hurt. I nod towards the bottle. "Scar, pour us another glass. We're gonna need it."

She reaches over to the side table, clutches the epitome of French perfection, and empties the rest into our glasses. She closes her eyes, sips from the overfilled rim, and makes an *mmmm* sound. When she looks at me again, the sassy chick is back.

"Ooh girl, that is some good shit. I feel right as fuckin rain now. I think I just needed a minute. Those last deaths were all different kinds of icky." She pops her shoulders and wiggles her body, as if to try and forget the gruesome images.

I laugh on the inside, but shake my head on the outside. I can tell she's hiding her happiness through humor, which is not very nice. These poor guys! She says she's grossed out, but she's secretly ecstatic three more are gone for good. I just know it.

Scarlett jumps onto my lap, wraps her arms around me, and buries her face between my head and neck. In a soft whisper against my ear, she starts talking.

"It's okay not to be okay with this. You're right, I'm not gonna puke." She pauses. "Anymore." Then nods in certainty before continuing. "I'm sorry for ignoring how serious this moment must be for you. Being tipsy and making it about me probably isn't helping. It can be about you again. Okay, go. The floor is yours."

Oh, how generous of her. I can feel my eyes roll. She should know by now that I am completely used to her wanting a permanent spotlight. The truth is—I don't mind. It takes a lot of drama off me and gives people the impression that I'm the calmer, more approachable one. Which, sometimes, isn't true at all. With the arm that is free, I give her a few light pats on the back. I look at the screen and see 2, 3, and 4 lifeless.

Was the way they went humane? No. But I think their deaths had to be tougher because my hold of them was stronger. Whatever the reason may be, I feel happier. I can't see them in my head anymore, and maybe that frees up some space for more important things, like skinny jeans and designer handbags.

"I'm okay with this. I don't need a hug. We don't need to make this a big thing. I needed to let them go. It was harder than the first two, but it felt even more satisfying. Like I just ate a delicious molten lava cake without adding any calories!"

She sits up, still on my lap, and looks into my eyes. "But Henry was your first love!"

I shrug. "He was the first boy I said *I love you* to, though I'm not sure I actually ever meant it."

Scarlett gasps. "*Quelle surprise!*" She gives an over-dramatic inhale.

I was just a teen, what did she expect? "He was kind of a bad boy, with the drinking and partying and tattoos and all, but behind that hid a proper Catholic boy. He wouldn't do me doggy style until *love* was involved." I'm not a Saint, that's a fact.

Scarlett sits on her knees. "So you lied? For sex? You're my hero." We clink our glasses in cheers. "So is that why you let him believe he was your first?"

She got me! There's no hiding the rest, so I may as well tell it like it is. I was young and made a very misguided decision to humor his ideals so I could get what I wanted. She is probably only proud because she's done the same thing—only she may not have the excuse of being a naive adolescent at the time. Who knows?

"I liked him a lot, I really did, and I thought, well, maybe it will grow into love soon, so why not. After I got a taste of cherry pie with Chad, I couldn't go cold turkey off deserts. A girl's gotta eat."

We both lift up our arms for a high five.

I feel my abs crunching from the laughter inside. "But come on, Scar, it can't really be so much of a shock considering how easy it was for me to leave him."

Henry and I met in university. He was a few years older than me, absolutely smitten, but I was more or less just anxious to be in a grown-up relationship. We were together for a little over a year, though it felt like thirty years. Not a good sign. He was really friendly with my mates and got close with my family, especially my brother, which I liked.

One day while I was visiting my family in San Francisco, I went out with my sister and met Number 3.

A light bursts on Scarlett's face as she recalls the break-up. "Oh ya, you felt guilty about getting naked with Alec so you sent Henry a text message letting him know it was 'okay to have fun' while you were away."

We both laugh.

Not my classiest move. In fact, Scar and our friend Ivey teamed up with my sisters and gave me a metaphorical trophy for worst break-up line in history. It took four years for someone to beat it. The new title owner is Ivey's ex-boyfriend who tweeted at her, *took the tomato plants and moved out #freedom.* That one makes mine seem polite.

When I recover my breath, I pause and sigh. "Oh, the cowardly things we did when we were younger. At least we can look back and laugh about it now."

Scarlett nods. "Ya, I'm not so sure he is laughing about it. The poor kid was so confused. And it didn't help that when you got back to Cambridge, you completely shut off your emotions towards him like a cold ice queen."

Ignoring the insult because it is the truth, I counter with another fact. "You would have, too, if you saw Number 3 naked. Alec was all I could think about. That ass was like a fucking sculpture."

Scarlett looks up to the ceiling, probably wishing she'd seen him in the nude, then brushes it off. "Still, I remember Henry being so shocked and hurt when you told him there was someone else that he started crying like you told him you were dying. Seeing a really tall man cry is strange. When they buckle down, they have so far to fall."

I look up and down, picturing it happen. A chuckle breaks out. "But actually, Henry was more than a foot taller than me. Giant. In his pants, too." I sigh. "He did cry a lot. He stayed in the denial phase for a few weeks, came over for dinner a few times, and kept talking to my brother on the telephone as if everything was normal."

Scarlett nods emphatically. "You played along. But after about three weeks, he moved straight into the anger phase and stayed there for a long time. He even tried to grab my boobs one night while he was plastered at a pub."

Ya, that sounds like something he would do. And by tried, I bet she meant it really did happen, but without her consent. He always got handsy when he drank. My mother personally witnessed it when he grabbed her butt on the dance floor at my cousin's wedding. My dad brushed it off as a joke, but secretly liked him less after that. I raise my glass to show acquiescence. "Well, his overly excessive drinking no doubt drowned his pain."

She speaks with her hand flipping side to side. "So you remained attached to him because you felt responsible for his downward spiraling behavior after you left him? Or maybe it was the guilt for cheating on him? Or could it be you feel a little blame for him being married and divorced twice since you?"

I smile and playfully slap her wrist. "Ouch! Three jabs in one sentence. You're on a roll!"

She puts her hands on my face and her voice drips with sympathy. "I guess there were a few reasons to hold on to him."

Well, if you count the guilt of cheating, of lying for sex, of pretending to love him, and from the confusing break-up text, then ya, I guess there were some. But they all boiled down to one thing: guilt. Realizing my leg was losing feeling from Scarlett's Kardashian-like ass, I take her hand off my face and push her off my lap.

She swivels over to her own lounge chair without a fuss.

I look over at her and put on my Mamma Green voice to better convey my sincerity. "For a while, I actually erased Henry from my memory because of the guilt I buried somewhere deep inside me. When I tried to recall moments we had together, I simply couldn't remember, as if I had amnesia."

I shrug. "Tonight, I realized that the only way to let Henry go was to open my heart and release the responsibility and guilt I bore, and forgive myself."

I huff. That was harder to admit out loud than in my head. I take a large sip of the overfilled glass of red liquid painkiller.

Scarlett rolls her eyes. "Alex, that was the only time you've ever been unfaithful! Our judgment was not exactly clear when we were that young. No one's is. This is what people call life lessons. We are supposed to learn from them or something. So what, you learned it almost ten years later, and by metaphorically killing him, everyone deals with things in their own way. You are a good person."

Feeling uplifted by her unconventional pep talk, I smile and burrow into the seat. "Letting go of my guilt was the best feeling I've had all night! I feel a glow in my cheeks, and it's not from the wine. It's from the restored faith I have in myself."

Henry is gone, out of my heart and in a better place.

Interrupting my own reflection time, I point out, "Are we going to ignore the fact that two other guys were just killed?"

Chapter Sixteen

Sailing the Sea of Exes

We both burst into laughter. My giggle lingers a little longer—bouncing off the giant windows and silver leafed ceiling in the impeccably posh lounge.

Scarlett snidely remarks, "I wasn't really a part of the Alec and Rob era. You were more or less on your own for those ones, so yes, I ignored their deaths."

I put down my glass. How did she not see the poetry of it all? "What? I think Alec was an epic death. He was the reason I left Henry, so it was fitting to have them die together, and Josh taking Alec's life because he was always so unnecessarily jealous of him was appropriate, too. I thought you would like the linkage."

She crosses her arms. "You want me to appreciate Alec's death? I can do that. He was an idiot and complete waste of your time."

"Tell me how you really feel," I sarcastically jab back.

This is what I was talking about earlier regarding Scarlett. She is a hater of most of my exes because they took me away from her even for a short amount of time. But she hates Alec for different reasons. Her extremely high level of hatred, though, has no justification.

She uncrosses her arms to take a big gulp of Merlot, then sets it down, places her hands one over the other, and props her body on it's side, towards me. "You met Alec after his first pro game which happened to be in San Fran. He won. He thought of you as a good luck charm. He banged your brains out. He knocked up some bitty a few months later. Begged you to take him back. Then married the baby mamma. Oldest story in the book. You can move on now. Josh killed him."

I clap my hands and shake my head. How has this woman not yet realized that none of these guys can be swept under the rug so easily? She's so thick-headed. Alec may have not been her favorite dude, but he's not an easy one to get over; he's the only guy to ever cheat on me. That's heavy shit! "Well, thank you for closing that case so quickly, Sherlock. Would you mind giving me at least one minute to talk it out?"

Scarlett pouts and huffs. "Ugh. Fine. But the guy thought California was a part of Canada. That is all I have to say about him."

She has a point. He was dumb. But when you look like he does, and make as much money, intelligence matters a lot less. Wow, that sounded really shallow. Oh well, it was the truth. I lean towards her. "If Alec would have been mute and faithful, we would have had the perfect relationship. It was casual, fun, and exactly what I needed after leaving Henry."

Scar shoots me her *you gotta be kidding me* face—which mostly consisted of a raised brow and a half smile-before she throws her hands up in the air and blurts, "Except he was a religious southern American boy, a Republican, he used to eat pot brownies for breakfast, and he didn't take his amazing career seriously. Oh, and he sleeps with every opened leg in sight!"

Another wave with my glass. "I was about to say, except we had absolutely nothing in common." Holy mother, will I ever get to finish a sentence around this blabber mouth?

She surprisingly doesn't respond.

Was she out of witty comments? That would be a first! Wow, I'm sounding like a real bitter bitch. The truth is, I wasn't mad that Alec and I didn't work out. I mean, the simple thought of having to deal with people saying, *this is Alec's wife, Alex,* for the rest of my life was excruciating enough. I sigh. "In all honesty, Alec and I had so much fun together. But I never had any real feelings for him because I was still blocked from the built-up guilt from Henry."

Scarlett drops the tough girl act and reaches her hand out to mine in a gesture of sympathy and understanding.

I can feel my eyelashes flutter, my way of trying to contain my emotions. Cheating on Henry actually hurt me more than being cheated on by Alec. I was hardly upset with him at all. I was more disappointed in myself for trying to force something that clearly was not going to happen—a future together. I compose myself with a deep inhale and turn to her.

"I think I gave him a real chance because I had hopes that I could be the strong wife behind the busy athlete, like my mother to my father. I was obviously way off with this one. I guess it's true that women are attracted to men that remind them of their fathers."

Ew. Saying "attracted" and "father" in the same sentence will never sound right.

"I needed to admit to myself that I always knew, not so deep down, that Alec and I weren't meant to be." A reality-check is a powerful healing tool. I should try using it more often.

My mom and dad are an inspiration, but I guess I didn't need to translate their love so literally. It was an innocent twenty-one year-old's mistake. I am not going to be Alec's wife, and that's okay, because I'm pretty fuckin happy without him. Being strong and supportive of my own endeavors has been working out smashingly.

I turn to Scar. "There are no regrets with this one. He's officially out of my head. And, I have to say, it feels awesome!"

Going back to her sarcastic self, Scarlett reminds me, "You may have held on to a small amount of feelings for Alec, but you never spoke to him again after Spring Break in Hawaii when you met Number 4."

"Rob, aka Tarzan, would have had that effect on anyone."

I stick my nose into the top of my glass and take a deep breath in. The smell of fruit always takes me back to the thought of islands and white sandy beaches.

Scarlett frowns and taps her finger on her lip while pondering. "I'm actually surprised you are able to let go of Kumbaya Rob so soon. He was your *one that got away,* wasn't he?"

I smile as her nickname for him flitters in memories of him singing that around a campfire with us one night. Earlier that same day, he caught some fish with his bare hands and decided to show us what a real island barbeque tasted like. He always loved getting groups together and making people smile with some fresh food and cheesy hippie music. He hunted, cooked, sang pretty well, and had abs you could wash clothes on. If that doesn't make any girl want to take their panties off immediately, something is wrong with them.

I tilt the glass and watch the liquid move back and forth, reminding me of ocean waves.

She must've noticed me drifting away with a smile on my face. "Are you daydreaming about Rob? I'm right here."

I put my hand over my mouth and giggle like a schoolgirl, then recall my time with him out loud. "Rob and I immediately had an intense, undeniable, and unexplainable connection, as if we were lovers in a past life.

He would look straight into my eyes and I would be hypnotized. We were attached at the hip for the entire vacation."

She leans towards me with one eyebrow arched. "I remember. I was there, too. Not that you acknowledged me."

For a second, I almost forgot everything had to be about her. How silly of me. I shake my head, smiling. "Oh whatever, you spent the whole vacation with what's-his-name."

I hold my hand up to stop Scar from jumping in. She sits back in submission, then I continue, "Rob and I had so many adventures. Surfing, climbing, hiking, scaling waterfalls, skinny dipping in fresh water pools, eating strange foods, and we even watched a cock fight with the locals."

That was a strange event. Not only was it brutal and disgusting, but it also smelled really bad. Participating in illegal sports definitely doesn't require a high level of personal hygiene. I feel my face scrunch with judgment.

Putting aside recent events, Rob was always such a gentle guy. When I returned to Cambridge after spring break, we talked every day and rang up an impossibly high phone bill. Three weeks later, he asked me to come back to Hawaii and live with him for the summer because he couldn't bear to ever be without me again.

He was like a dream. He did and said things that you only read in love poems.

Scarlett claps her hands to bring me back to earth, as I seemed to have floated away into my thoughts again.

She props her hand on her hip. "As soon as the semester was over, you flew back to Hawaii to be with him. I was always skeptical and I could have told you something was off with this guy."

I squint at her. "Would you like to commence your *I told ya so* dance now?"

She shrugs and rolls her eyes simultaneously.

What? She's all of a sudden above that kind of thing? Just a few days ago, I witnessed our friend Ivey having to endure it. Ivey was hitting on her yoga instructor every day for five weeks, even though Scarlett insisted he was gay. Scar was right and the dance lasted a whole two minutes.

I shouldn't count my eggs just yet—she may be holding out for a later dude's death. But since she doesn't seem to be moving any time soon, I'll continue. I cross my arms and tilt my chin up. "I flew to Hawaii and spent an amazing week with Rob. He introduced me to his friends, took me on more adventures, and told me he loved me."

Scarlett rolls her eyes again. Avoiding having to verbally comment, she buries her face in her wine. Her eye roll said more than enough.

She seems to be giving me a generous amount of airtime. I wonder why, though, best not to ask and just keep on while I can. "I remember calling my mother one night and telling her I thought Rob was *the one*. I was only twenty one and had pretty much told her every guy I met was *the one*. So sue me, I was a romantic. My mom responded, 'That's nice, sweetie. We'll be in Argentina next week for Dad's race. Come and be with us, you're bound to find a soul mate there, too.' She was probably not wrong."

"Mothers know best," Scarlett mutters under her breath as she plays with her hair, showing me she is bored of the conversation.

Well, that's why she's letting me talk—just to get this convo over with! She's not as sneaky as she thinks, I see straight through her act. But I think it's best for her to hear this too, I'm not sure she knows what all really happened. Honesty is my newest policy. Let's see how long it can stick.

I loosen my smile. "The next morning, I woke up to a man that was not Rob on the deck drinking coffee. He was Rob's sponsor. He told me that Rob was a recovering addict and was not stable enough to start a relationship with anyone. Rob was apparently in recovery for only two months when I met him. He was previously addicted to cocaine, meth amphetamines, alcohol, ecstasy, oxycodone, and more. That day, I got on a plane and returned to London. He called three or four times over the next year with wildly delusional ideas of us running away together to Mexico, Indonesia, and Bali. I finished university, moved towns, changed my number, and never heard from Rob again."

Scarlett stops playing with her hair, the look of shock on her face. "Whoa. That's some shit. Did you even get to see Rob before you left Hawaii?"

I throw my hand up in the air. "No! His sponsor escorted me to the airport. Like I was some sort of fugitive." I drop my hand and feel my brows lift. "He was actually kind of cute, you would have been into him."

She makes her sexy face, pursing out her lips and fluttering her eyelashes.

She must be fishing for a compliment as she's holding her look for more than enough time. I give in and lean towards her. "Yes, he would have been into you, too."

"Obviously." She smiles and whips her head around, making her hair fall perfectly over her shoulders. "I think I get it. Your continued attachment to Tarzan was because you never had proper closure."

Bingo.

"Exactly. But tonight I realized that the only reason I held on to the thought of being with Rob was because I wanted to be the one to save him. I know, that whole controlling thing coming back into play. I'm learning."

Scarlett sympathetically nods. "You can't save an addict. An addict needs to save himself."

If only I didn't have to learn that the hard way-with a bruised heart. I feel tears welling up in my eyes. "I know that now."

I must have thought about him at least once a month for the past seven years. I wished I could talk to him again. See how he is doing and hope he has fully recovered. The not knowing part is what kept me holding on. But it's over, and has been since the day his sponsor made me leave.

As cruel as it sounds, his well being is not my responsibility and if we really are connected in some sort of cosmic way, letting him go will probably help him, too.

I shut my eyes and try to remember him, but all I see is a bird soaring in the air. A warm feeling flows through my body like an ocean wave.

Goodbye, Rob.

Scarlett raises her glass and toasts. "To important realizations, releases, and the half-way point!"

After wiping my tears, I sniffle, shake my emotions away, and sit up straight.

I reach over to Scar, clink glasses, then shove the sweet red nectar into my face.

Chapter Seventeen

Medieval Shit

Back on the rooftop, everybody is frozen still as if a pause button had been pressed.

Josh, standing behind the chair that was once occupied by the living version of Alec.

Clint, kneeling behind the bar on his way to standing back up.

Sebastian, leaning over the counter and catching a glimpse of Rob on the floor.

Liam, sitting on the bar stool with his head down.

The play button is pressed and each man takes a deep breath in.

Within milliseconds, Liam presses his right foot into Rob's lifeless body then takes his right hand and peels the axe out of the bloodied skull. He brings his left hand to support the base of the axe and moves his right one, near the blade. He lifts the tool behind his back and over his shoulder, way above his head. "Ahhhhhh!"

Clint pops up to see what is happening. His eyes widen immediately. His heart drops to his feet and he instinctually ducks for cover. Again.

Josh, still under the high of the adrenaline rush of killing Alec, is blind to all that is around him.

Matteo, just a few steps away from Liam, turns to his left, grabs Josh, and pulls them both to the floor.

Sebastian looks up and takes his last breath.

With brute force and impeccable precision, Liam drives the axe into Sebastian's head.

Sebastian's eyes blink once, twice, and then stay open. Blood drips over his face.

Liam pulls the axe out and the two hundred pounds of solid muscle thump to the floor.

Sebastian, Number 8, is dead.

Liam holds the axe in the air and screams, "Does anybody else want to test me?"

***

Scarlett and I find ourselves sitting on our knees in the lounge chairs with our wine glasses clutched in hand.

Scarlett lets out an escalating, "W…wha…whaat?" Her stutter subsides. "Man, that was badass!"

I smile with my whole face. My eyebrows start to tilt a little and my smile stretches to a deviously mischievous length.

We look over at each other. I keep smiling.

Scarlett jumps out of her seat, puts her glass down.

I lean back and blink as she lunges towards me.

She hops onto my seat and grabs my shoulders with both hands. "That. Was. Awesome."

I shake my head but can't seem to stop smiling.

Scarlett continues, "That is some Spartacus shit right there. Liam is a god. He literally pulled an axe out of two dead guys' heads within one minute. That can't be easy. Skulls are thick."

I nod, as she doesn't give me much room to do anything else. "The yelling with the axe over the head part was my favorite. Ugh. So manly."

Scarlett is so close to me, I can feel her breath on my face as she exclaims, "So manly."

We both sigh.

She lets go of my shoulders and stands up, facing the screen. "But poor Liam was the one who wanted to figure things out peacefully." She turns and waves her hand, gesturing for me to come stand beside her. "He thought if no one hurt each other, you would get bored and give in. Why have him go all Rambo now?"

"That side of him was boring me." In a valley girl voice, I continue while twirling my hair. "Ooooh, Liam is so sweet and naive I could just jump in his pocket and have him carry me around wherever he goes."

Scarlett rolls her eyes. "If you think that was an impression of me, you are about to get slapped."

I laugh. She doesn't.

"No, I wasn't saying it was you. Maybe this lesson isn't about my exes; maybe it's about trying to get you to realize that not everything is about you."

I laugh again. She doesn't.

I grab her arm and shake it. "Oh, come on."

She breaks. "Well, besides the fact that I now hate you, I agree. Liam was being too optimistic and he really does have a dark side and I'm glad you showed it."

I let her go and pat her on the back. "That's my girl."

Finally recognizing the bigger revelation from recent events, Scarlett lifts her hand, showing me her palm, and bluntly states, "So Sebastian is dead."

I high-five her open palm. "Yep. Super dead."

She laughs. "Okay, I gotta say this. I don't actually know who Sebastian is."

She does know who he is, kind of. I nod, a little embarrassed. "Ah yes, because I never referred to him by his first name."

She smiles. "So you're taking a page from me now?"

I twist my bottom lip as I think. "No, actually. Remember that rule we learned from our friend Ivey?"

She lifts her finger in the air. "The one about pulling out?"

"No." I shake my head, hoping Scar doesn't actually believe in the statistics Ivey shared—that it is eighty seven percent effective as birth control. It's not.

She brings her hand up a little higher. "The one about never trusting twins?"

"No." I cross my arms not actually knowing that one. Was it about twins pretending to be each other, or simply not trusting them because they are a genetic phenomena? I wouldn't put it past Ivey to accuse twins of being aliens.

Scar extends her arm almost completely. "Oh, the one about vacation flings not counting as cheating?"

"No!" I pull her arm down and chuckle. I think the rapper Ludacris made that one up, but his wording was something like *a new ho in every zip code*. Same thing.

I keep a grip of her hand, encouraging her to listen. "The rule she taught us was to give every guy we date a nickname. That way, the moment you start using his real name instead of his nickname, is when you know you've started to develop feelings for him."

Scarlett shakes out of my grasp. "Yes, I remember. Great rule. One of her smartest. Wise woman, that Ivey is."

"Ha. Maybe we should set her up with Matteo."

We both chuckle as we imagine what that train wreck would look like.

I digress. I grab both of our Merlots and hand Scar's to her. "Well, you don't know Sebastian's name because we always called him Arian Gorilla, which quickly short-formed to A-Go."

Scarlett remembers. "Oh! Haha. Sebastian is A-Go? That makes more sense now. But you never had feelings for him, so why hold on to him for so long?"

I answer bluntly. "Sex."

She chokes as she laughs with a mouthful of happy juice. "You're a slut. This is the second guy you've held on to because of sex."

What did she want me to say? That I held onto him for his impeccable culinary skills? No. I don't even think he owned utensils. More accurately, I don't know if he owned forks or knives because we never ate. "Scar, we never even had dinner together. There wasn't enough time. Being naked was our main priority. After all, what did I say every time he texted me?"

She moves her glass away from her face to answer before taking another sip. "It's a go."

"And what did that mean?" I smile.

She thrusts her hips and humps the air. "Sex time."

See. She knew who he was all along.

I laugh. "His penis was made for my vagina and I just didn't know how to let that go. Our genitals were soul mates."

She raises her brow. "Wasn't he the guy that wore your panties over his head during sex?"

I awkwardly pause while I watch the last drop empty out of my glass. Once again. I must be very thirsty.

I answer while glancing around for a new bottle. "Yes. And in my defense, I did not know that was so strange until I mentioned it to you."

Scarlett shakes her head. "He was more than strange. He made a whole whack of money but didn't own a bed. He slept on the floor."

I'm not sure how clearer I need to be about this? "It didn't matter to me. We never slept." I get up and search the room for an unopened import. An empty glass just doesn't feel right.

She shouts as she takes a seat. "The guy made you watch Japanese anime during sex once."

"Actually, twice," I correct as I return with a 2000 Bordeaux. The best year for it, in my opinion.

She purses her lips together, making a kissing noise. "Yes, please." She downs the rest of the red delicious and lifts her arm for a refill. "Not that my point hasn't already been made, but, he demanded you wear heels even while naked. You do realize that this guy treated you like a prostitute, right?"

Did she just throw out the hooker card? That is going right back into her face. "I'm not the one who contemplated being a prostitute," I jab as I fill her glass only half full.

She clears her throat and eyes me to continue pouring. "Hey, they make a lot of money and get shiny gifts."

Aha. Knew it. I shake my head as I take my seat. "You're delusional. But you're right. Sebastian was not okay in the head and I never thought he was, but we can agree that a perfect penis is hard to let go."

Scarlett nods. "Agreed."

I smell the vintage Bordeaux. Flowers start to dance on my senses. What do I actually like more, sex or wine? I scratch my head. Tough call.

I turn to Scar and see her eyes closed and mouth seemingly sealed shut. I should serve her some of this more often.

I wait until she comes back to reality. "You feel that? That is how he made me feel. Pure satisfaction. So no, I never took Sebastian seriously as someone to settle down with, but despite the uncontrollable physical attraction, I did stop saying yes to dates with him. Though it was super duper hard."

Scarlett smiles, keeping her focus on the liquid satisfaction. "How very mature of you."

I lean over and wave my hand in front of her face to bring her thoughts back to the task at hand. "When he realized it was over, he didn't take no for an answer—a genuine businessman and a true German. I allowed him to see me one last time while out for drinks. I told him it would be just as friends and we were not going to get naked."

She raises her eyebrows at me. "So you got naked?"

She knew me too well. I lift my hand and shrug. "So, we got naked."

We both smile in understanding.

I can't get anything past this girl. "I realized then that I had no self control when it came to him. I blamed it on my down-low brain. And do you remember what happened next?"

She pauses for a few seconds then gives me a devious smile. "I deleted his number from your phone."

That's right! She erased him as a contact so for the next few weeks I kept getting texts from an unknown number saying strange things—mostly about boobs—and I brushed it off as a wrong number. I nod aggressively. "Yes, and the next time I talked to him was two years later. The poor guy sent me an email saying he hates me a little bit for how easy it was for me to cut him off completely. He said I was the only girl he has ever had feelings for and referred to me as *the one that got away*."

Scarlett throws her hands up and dramatically says, "Sebastian is the most bizarre man in the world. It has been confirmed."

I catch myself picking at the material on the lounge chair. Why am I being so fidgety? I need to relax. I take a long inhale and place my hand flat on my knee. I know a relationship takes a lot more than sex and we didn't have what we needed for it to last. We didn't have balance. I want it all, not just the physical aspect.

Number 8 had to go.

"I will always remember the fun we had, *sans* clothes, but it's time for me to stop comparing that aspect of him to other men. After all, sex with love is always better than freaky deaky emotionally detached sex. It's harder to find, but it's the truth."

Sebastian's anger towards me will always be trapped in his larger than life ego, but my strings are no longer attached to him.

An exhale escapes my lungs. My shoulders drop and my posture softens.

Scarlett smiles as she realizes I just let another guy out.

I turn my focus to the flat screen, look at the events that have come to pass, and can't help but be proud of myself.

Scar takes my hand and looks into my eyes. "Let's keep going. You can do this. I know you can."

I look back into hers and grip firmly. A smile forces its way through my cheeks. I feel touched.

She then ruins the moment. "Plus I'm dying to get back to the testosterone-driven Spartans." She pops her shoulders. "Mmm. Mmm."

I wave my wine towards her. "Cheers to that!"

Chapter Eighteen

Choices

The blood pumping in Liam's veins make the blue lines bulge through the skin on his face and has him look angrier than ever. He holds the axe in the air and waits for a response to his rhetorical question.

The still adrenaline-pumped Josh and Matteo quickly rise to their feet and run to the opposite side of the rooftop, as far away from Liam as possible.

Clint pops up from behind the bar with his hands in the air signaling his surrender. He looks over at Liam and pleads, "Listen man, I am innocent here. I haven't killed anyone. I'm on your side, bud. Those guys are psychos. Didn't you see the absence of humanity in their eyes?"

An intimidating amount of air fills Liam's chest.

Clint's hands tremble as he gets more nervous.

Liam drops the axe and huffs. "No, I didn't. I was too busy getting strangled."

Clint relaxes a little and lowers his hands, then lies. "I had nothing to do with that. I swear."

Liam rubs his neck. "I don't believe you."

Clint holds his hand to his chest. "I could never kill anyone, not even if my life depended on it."

That was the truth.

Liam scowls. "I know you could never pull the trigger, but that doesn't mean you couldn't give the order."

Clint raises his arms as if surrendering to the police. "I don't blame you for not trusting me."

Pointing at Josh and Matteo, he continues. "But those killers won't hesitate to come after you again."

Liam agrees but does not respond and grips the corner of the bar top, trying to release some anger from his body.

Clint drops his fist on the counter and looks confidently into his eyes. "I say we stick together and create a strategy that results in both of us living."

Liam's heart's pace slows down. His head feels clearer. Leaving the axe on the floor, he walks behind the bar and right up to Clint.

Clint freezes.

Liam extends his hand.

Clint straightens his posture, looks down, and realizes his peace offering has worked. He has successfully joined forces with the guy who has the only weapon around. Clint takes Liam's hand, looks into his eyes like a proper lawyer, and convincingly says, "You can trust me."

Liam holds his fierce scowl. "You've got a deal."

Huddled closely on the opposite side of the room, Josh and Matteo immediately start to strategize.

Matteo breathes heavily, trying to control his heart rate. He looks over at the bar. "Clint has flipped on us. We need to kill him."

Josh nods in agreement with one hand on Matteo and the other on his chest, feeling his lungs puff in and out.

Matteo turns to Josh. "Liam has an axe and some sort of combat training. My pocketknife is no match and a fistfight is also out of the question. We need to think out of the box. Catch them off guard. And do it quick."

Josh's eyes light up as he remembers. "I know where an arrow is. I just don't know where there is a bow."

Matteo grins and pats Josh on the back. "I'm a hunter. I can hit any target within a hundred meter radius. Easily. Show me this arrow."

Josh pops his head up and looks around the room to remember which ledge he found it under. He thinks to himself, *opposite to the side where Chad went down and to the right of the pissing corner. That should be where it is. Holy shit. That's beside us.*

Josh leans back and stretches his arm out and to the left. Matteo watches him try to discretely reach under the ledge.

"Aha." Josh pulls the arrow down and hides it behind his back. "Here it is. But it is useless without a bow."

Matteo looks at the arrow and sees the tip is made of titanium. Heavy but lethal. He sternly looks at Josh.

"No weapon is useless."

Ideas spin through his MacGyver-like mind. *I can use the lighting wire and a leg from the barstool. The wire may not be elastic enough. The metal leg may take too long to rip off. I can take apart another lounge chair and see what materials we have to work with. Too long. Fuck it. We need to find a bow. She must have hidden both parts. She couldn't have only given us an arrow. She was mischievous but not cruel. There is a bow somewhere. But where?*

Matteo lies on his back and looks up.

Josh lies beside him.

Josh turns his head and realizes how uncomfortable close he is to Matteo's face. He shuffles sideways and whispers, "What's the plan?"

Matteo answers while maintaining his focus on the task at hand. "To find the bow. Spin your body around and look under every ledge. It's too risky to be walking too close to the opposition. We need to stay in this spot. The bow will be strung with wire that will glisten a little if the light hits it just right. Look for something that is reflecting."

Josh copies Matteo, pointing his arms out, trying to focus his vision at the end of his fingertips. They look like a pair of eight-year-olds trying to make snow angels in the summer.

Matteo squints and points. "There."

Josh gets up to his knees and leans towards Matteo. "There where?"

Matteo doesn't respond. His mind is focused on the adjacent corner. His heart races a little faster. He gets to his feet and squats down to be able to see under the ledge. He takes four wide steps, closes his eyes, reaches his hand under the concrete ledge, and prays. His eyes open suddenly. He grabs his pocketknife and makes two swift cuts. He stands straight with his back towards Clint and Liam and pulls the bow to his chest.

Josh looks over and smiles. His smile glows through his body, filling him up with hope and optimism.

Matteo walks back over to Josh and puts his hand out asking for the arrow.

Josh places the arrow in Matteo's hand and nods as a silent *good luck.*

At the bar, Clint and Liam decide whether to attack the other two by rushing them and catching them off guard, or waiting to see if they can come to some sort of truce.

Clint decides. "Surprise is all we have. You run at them with the axe and I will follow with a stool. Once you kill one, I will have knocked the other down, giving you the advantage. Teamwork. All we need to remember is to not get too close to Matteo. He has a knife."

Clouded with adrenaline, Liam agrees to the plan. "I will rush Matteo. You get Josh."

Clint nods.

The two stand side by side and move their bodies to the simultaneous count to three. "One, two…" They take a deep breath in, and sprint.

Matteo plants his feet firmly into the ground, holds the arrow, and connects it to the bow. He turns around, then on a long inhale, opens his eyes, and sees Liam charging at him with the axe.

Without a single ounce of panic, Matteo closes one eye to aim, exhales, and releases.

The arrow speeds almost invisibly through the midnight air, directly at Liam's chest. It pierces through his shirt, ribs, heart, and back.

Liam stops dead in his tracks. The axe drops out of his right hand. He grabs his chest and looks down to see the arrow. He feels shocked, confused, helpless and defeated.

Liam collapses to his knees then thumps to the ground on his side. His face lies on the cold concrete. He blinks to try and focus his attention. One last thought runs through his head. *I will see you soon, Mom.*

His eyes close and his heart stops beating.

Liam, Number 6, is dead.

Chapter Nineteen

Friend Zone

Scarlett embraces me as I begin to sob uncontrollably.

My head melts into her shoulder and tears start to cascade down her arm.

"I'm sorry, I don't know why I am so emotional. I just know that he is such a good man. And he loves his mother. Every man who loves his mother is a good man in my eyes."

Scarlett laughs as she lifts me away from her and wipes my face with a tissue from the side table. "You are truly a mess, Alexandria."

Does she think she's helping by saying that? Boy, tough love is a real bitch. I feel a laugh bubbling in my throat. I pat under my eyes to clear the running mascara away. With a sniffle and a smile, I push her off my chair.

"You're a jerk," I jab.

Scarlett stumbles up and bursts into laughter. She shoos my words away with a wave. "You just made Matteo kill Liam with an arrow through the heart. Like a moose." She plops down into her seat and moves her mouth, repeating the *ooh* sound, making her face look like a fish.

The bubble in my throat turns into full-blown laughter. "He kind of reminds me of a moose."

Our wine giggles echo loudly off the floor-to-ceiling windows.

I try to mellow myself with a sip of rich red, then turn to her. "But really, it was hard to let him go. Liam is my friend. *Our* friend, actually. He holds such an important place in my heart."

Scarlett places her glass down and smacks her lips together, showing how much she enjoyed the bold flavors. "He *is* our friend." She reaches over and holds my right hand. "The reason you needed to let him go was not because you still have romantic feelings for him. It was deeper than that."

What's she suggesting? It sure as hell isn't about sex. Liam is like a brother to me. I shake my head. "Well, diagnose me then, doctor."

She tilts her head and squints her whole face at me. "Alexandria, think about it. Who do you go to for male advice? Who have you compared the others to, on an emotional level, since him? And whom do you introduce anyone to right before you break up with them?

I feel my mouth drop to my chest in an exaggerated reaction to the accusations. "Listen, I love Liam, but I am not in love with him. Let's just get that out there."

Scarlett shakes her head. "You're talking with your hands, and when you're not Italian, it just makes you look like a drama queen."

I was? Oh, I was. I shove my hands into my armpits. Though, it's not really fair that she gets away with it and I can't. I've spent just as much time in her homeland as she has!

Scarlett grins. "You're an idiot. I am not saying you are in love with him. I am saying he is like a brother to you, and you can't compare someone you want to be with to your brother!"

I feel a very sassy eye roll coming on. "Duh." I tilt my head towards her and admit, "Actually, that is exactly what I just said in my head. He is like a brother to me." Hmm. My suspicions are rising. That's second time tonight. Maybe she really *is* a mind reader? Dear God, I hope not. Some things are definitely better left unknown. Like how her Louboutins got so scuffed or her new camera lens cracked. I'm happy with her assumption it was due to natural causes. Teehee.

Scarlett smiles and pops her shoulders. "We are too similar for our own good."

She was right. About both things. We do have a sisterly bond. And after we stopped dating, I kind of looked to Liam like an older sibling. He was the perfect big bro. He scared the bad boys away when I needed him to, he listened to my complaining and nagging without any judgment, and he actually answered honestly when I asked him if I looked too stumpy in certain dresses.

"Maybe I have been letting him intervene in my dating life too much. I never even gave Sebastian a chance because Liam said I should be with someone who has dinner with me and doesn't just eat dessert off me."

Scarlett chuckles. "That one shouldn't have to be pointed out."

I shrug and smirk, accepting that my past includes a few misguided decision-making moments. "I can't believe how freeing it feels to realize that an ex who is just a friend now was creating a block in my heart."

Scarlett tipsily waves her Bordeaux in the air and giggles. "Sometimes, you need to kill your ex to realize he was your ex."

I smile and pet her hair. "Scarface, thank you for doing this with me. I feel like we are making real progress."

She throws her hands in the air, minding her glass of course, and says, "Did you hear that? Progress, people!"

She hops out of her seat, kicks off her heels, and tiptoes over to the flat screen. She points at Clint. "Look at how shocked his face is! What do you think he is going to do now that he doesn't have Liam to defend him? Will he run and hide, or lawyer his way out of this?"

I lean down and gently peel my heels from my feet—they are too precious to kick off. I melt into the lounge chair and toss my arm up. "Let's find out."

Chapter Twenty

Giving Up

The room dissolves away as I stand up off the micro suede sofa and walk with my shoulders slouched and head down towards my bedroom.

Scarlett scrambles up, looking confused. "What are you doing? I thought we were going to find out what happens to the last few guys. Don't leave me hanging, man."

I continue on to my room without taking a pause to listen to her.

She uncrosses her legs, puts her wine down, and shuffles out of our big comfy couch. She scratches her head contemplating her next move. She nods to herself then picks the known soothing agent, grabs my glass, too, and follows me to the bedroom.

After crawling onto my too-soft-for-anyone's-liking bed, I pull my down pillow into my stomach and naturally form into it.

Scarlett stands in the doorway. "Dude, what is the sad face and fetal position about? I thought we were going to kill all of your exes. I was having fun."

I grunt. Can't she give me three goddamn seconds to wallow? A girl should be entitled to a significant amount of wallowing time after delving this deep into her emotions. I want my three seconds!

She walks towards the bed, sits down on the edge, and places the glass of wine in front of my nose. "You need more red delicious."

I roll onto my back, holding my knees and pillow to my stomach, then shut my eyes tight. Okay, that aroma isn't hurting the situation. But I still feel like being silent. I'll satisfy her with a lighter moan into these down feathers.

Scarlett sighs. "I can imagine how hard it must be to relive your failed relationships, even if just in your imagination."

Damn right it's tough. It feels like I'm tied to the front of a car in a high-speed chase, with the driver being admittedly a little drunk. Not ideal. Scar is in the helicopter above watching it all happen from a safe distance. She's all comfy cozy when I'm vulnerable and in the emotional *danger zone*. I frown and groan deeper so she gets the hint that I don't want to talk right now.

She puts her mouth to my ear and grunts even louder. Sarcasm. "Oh come on, you big suck. It isn't like you to pout. You're a goddamn Green. Man up and start acting like one."

A smile cracks the side of my mouth. She sounds like my dad. In fact, she is very similar to my father. They both suggest solving any problem with wine and tough love. It always works, so I guess I can't argue with proven results.

I peek through one eye to see the glass of wine still in front of my face. I smile even bigger. Then I immediately turn it back into a frown, hoping Scar didn't notice. I can't give in just yet; I am enjoying the safety of this spot right here too much. No exes in my sight or my mind.

Scarlett bounces on the mattress. "Aha! A smile. I saw it!"

Busted.

I open my eyes, aggressively grab the glass of wine, and sit up with my back to the headboard. I may as well continue drinking. I have a feeling it's about to get real sappy up in here. The last men standing obviously have a tougher hold of me.

Scarlett pokes the middle of my forehead.

She can't be pointing out my frown lines, can she?

She rubs a little deeper. "Yup. That's gonna need Botox soon."

She was! Way to kick a friend while she's down. I shake my head then shove my face until it's almost fully covered by the balloon glass of wine, then snarl, "You're a jerk."

She raises her hands in the air. "She speaks!"

"Har, har." I scowl.

Having no patience for my feel-sorry-for-me attitude, she claps her hands in front of my face. "Alexandria Lou Green, get your shit together. You can do this."

I turn my head away and pull the pillow in tighter. "But why? It was hard enough reflecting on the past seven guys."

I stop to ponder a point. At twenty-eight, I have seven-plus exes. That's normal, right? Then I shrug. Of course it is! I'm a young, liberated woman set out to conquer the world. Stockpiling hearts is really all in a day's work for my kind. Our friend Ivey is already on number twenty-six. Dating only ten men since I turned eighteen—totally normal. I could even be nominated for sainthood.

I glance back at my best friend. "It's past midnight and I think we've had three, maybe four bottles?" I look to her for an answer.

She shakes her head, having no idea.

I shrug. "Well, anyways, we've consumed a lot of French perfection. Let's just call it a day and continue another night."

With attitude in her voice, Scarlett counters with a swing of her head. "Well, Grandma, it's twelve twenty-five and crushing three bottles is like a regular Tuesday night to us. Like the great R. Kelly once said, *'It's the freakin weekend baby; I'm about to have me some fun'*. And I can't think of anything more fun than brutally killing all of your exes. Metaphorically, of course."

I smile. "I believe he also said, *This is the remix to ignition…*"

Scarlett joins in and like proper white girls, we rap the whole R Kelly *Ignition* song while bouncing up and down on my bed, wine in one hand and an east side or west side gang sign formed on the other hand. Who knows which one? We are so very gangster. Not.

After we finish botching the entirety of the R&B track, we burst out laughing.

I turn to Scarlett while taking another sip. "I'm not sure I can do this, Scar. I'm afraid to let everyone go. If I do, then I have nothing left to hold on to."

Scarlett understandingly nods and reaches her arm out to tuck my hair behind my ear. "That's the point, Alexandria. You can't move forward if you are holding on to the past." Then she smiles and jokes. "Basic laws of motion. And everyone knows you can't argue with science. Except for the religious nuts, and the Bermuda Triangle, I suppose." Her gaze wanders into space.

Trying to avoid the sentimental talk, I shake out my wavy brown locks, grab a section, and start inspecting my dead ends. I may be acting like a child, but this is an emotional workout. I probably haven't cried this much since I was an infant. And not surprisingly, the outcome remains the same—I want my mommy.

Scarlett rubs my leg. "I think I'm seeing the purpose of this exercise now. No matter how deep the feelings were or how long a relationship may have been, it is a human being's life that you were a part of. A living, breathing, laughing, loving, real person."

That makes me think of the first time Josh told me he loved me. I came down for breakfast and he had spelled it out on the table with Cheerios. Then he said "my love for you is as real and wholegrain as this breakfast cereal." His adorable Irish accent made his words even funnier, but it still made me cry.

Is that what Scar is trying to do? Make me cry more? Her hand on my leg is soothing me but I can still feel my chin starting to tremble.

She inches closer to me as she sees me well-up.

My face instinctually leans into her hand as she cups my cheek. She smiles. "And like the butterfly effect, everything you touch has an impact on the future. For you, these men were all steps to where you are now."

I shut my eyes and feel each breath flow in and out of my lungs.

Scarlett brings my face to her bosom. "And where you are now is a mentally strong, physically weak, beautiful, funny, intelligent, and successful woman. Sure, you're a little crazy, but who isn't. Your past experiences contributed to the awesome chick you are today. You don't need to hold on to them to be that. But you need to release them so your future awesome dude can be let in."

Buried in her large breasts but feeling too comfortable to move, I listen to her heartbeat. *Thump, thump, thump.*

Her words resound through each pulse. I am a strong woman. And I'm in control of my own happiness. It is I who can make myself feel complete, not these lingering thoughts or moments from my past. I open my eyes and glance at my hot pink colored toenails.

I am an independent kick ass chick—it's time I start acting like one.

I drink the last sip of my dark liquid mistress. I place the empty glass down on the side table and tackle-hug Scarlett.

She falls back, nearly hitting her head on the headboard. She looks up to her hand in the air clutching her glass. Saved were the last two sips of wine.

I smile and keep my arms wrapped tightly around her. "I love the shit out of you!"

I didn't need to say anything more. She knew that meant I was back to my regular self.

She pats my back. "I love the shit out of you, too, you crazy bitch. Can I have my body back now?"

I get off her, grab my glass, and return to the living room. Before I get there, I glance out the window and notice the sensor light turned on. Oh shit! The cat! I hurry towards the patio door and swing it open; thinking Vera desperately wants to come in. Nope. She's happily plopped on the corked balcony flooring. I step out and tap her a little with my foot, encouraging her to come in. She sprints inside, down the hallway, and disappears into the darkness of my room. I sigh as I shut the door behind me. God, I wish I could join her.

Scarlett makes a stop to the loo, and grabs another bottle of wine on her way through the kitchen. She stops to pour the Cabernet Sauvignon into a decanter and carries it with her. "It's a multi-grape night," she hollers at me.

I take the decanter out of her hand as she reaches me. I don't trust her pouring, especially after confirming losing count of how many we've had. I take a sip. "Mmm. As long as it's French, I'm happy."

She nods.

We flop into our big beige sofa, cross our legs, and face each other.

"Ready?" I punctuate the question with a raised eyebrow.

Scarlett nods excessively. "Ready!" Her eyes widen with anticipation.

"Clink" toasts our glasses and with a blink, our San Francisco apartment disappears and we are returned to the posh lounge.

We sit like queens in our designer dresses and revert our attention back to the flat screen.

I pause, take a few deep inhales and repeat my mantra:

You can do this. You're a Green. Man up.
You can do this. You're a Green. Man up.
You can do this. You're a Green. Man up.

I elegantly lift my arm and decree, "Play".

Chapter Twenty-One

Instincts

The night seems darker than any night these men have ever seen.

Liam's cold, dead body lies stiff in the middle of the rooftop.

Still holding the stool in hand, Clint stands shocked, a foot away from death.

Josh smiles with satisfaction that he's chosen the right side.

A calm Matteo straightens his posture and tilts his head up with pride.

Matteo walks towards the body and gestures a Father, Son, and Holy Spirit. He looks down at Liam and certainty rings in his voice. "Quality shot. Clean and quick. He felt no pain." He kneels down and touches the body to show his respects. He thinks to himself, *you were a skilled and worthy opponent. May the gates of Heaven open for you.*

Clint's nerves heighten as he stares at Matteo, inches away from him.

Matteo looks up at Clint and calmly gestures towards his hand. "What are you planning to do with that chair, friend?"

Clint looks down at his grip and drops the stool immediately. "Ugh. Nothing. Nothing at all."

Josh walks over with a smug look on his face and tosses up his chin. "Yo, Matteo, what are you doing? Kill him. He deserves to die, that traitor." He spits on the ground.

Matteo stands up straight and turns towards Josh. He inhales deeply and closes his eyes.

Josh's cheeks get rosy from his frustration. He waits for Matteo to respond, but nothing happens. He frowns and points at Clint. "Fucking kill that motherfucker!"

Matteo sways confidently in front of Josh until their noses touch. His eyes widen. "Who the fuck do you think you are?"

Josh takes a step back and holds his hands out, claiming some distance.

Matteo takes a step forward and raises his brow. "You want Clint dead? Then you kill him."

Clint wants to run, but he can't. His heart starts to pound heavier as he uneasily waits for a reaction from Josh.

Unexpectedly, Josh breaks down and collapses onto the floor, sobbing. Like anything that gets too hot, he melts.

He looks up at Matteo with his eyes full of tears. "I'm so sorry. I just got caught up in the moment. I'm scared."

Clint lets out a relieved sigh.

Matteo tilts his head and softens his gaze. "What are you scared of?"

Josh throws his arms in the air upset at his unstable emotions. "I don't know. Dying, maybe? Never being able to see Alexandria again?"

Matteo kneels in front of Josh. "A secure man fears nothing."

Tears overflow Josh's eyes. "I'm not secure; I'm standing in a death trap without a way out. I'm not fuckin secure. I'm fuckin scared."

Matteo squints, strengthens his gaze, and repeats, "What are you scared of?"

Josh restlessly runs his fingers through his curls. "I'm afraid of letting Ally go. She was the love of my life. If I free her, then I end up empty."

Matteo puts his hands to Josh's chest. "Or, if you let her go, then you free yourself. And maybe, find someone who you can truly call the love of your life."

Josh holds Matteo's arm and leverages himself up to his knees. "You're right. I can't hold on to something I don't even have." He sniffs and wipes his running nose. "I need to be strong and let her go. I want her to find someone who makes her happier than I could." He stands up to his feet. "But I will always love her."

Matteo looks up at Josh and nods. "You make me proud."

Josh tilts his chin up, smirks, and walks towards the ledge. "A secure man fears nothing."

Josh's movement sparks curiosity in the boys' minds. They watch him like a hawk.

He climbs up on the ledge slowly and stands up straight. Avoiding looking forty stories down, he focuses on his chest expanding and contracting with each breath.

"Alexandria, if you can hear me, know that I am so grateful to have been a part of your life." He closes his eyes and brings his hands up to his heart. "You will make someone the luckiest man on Earth one day. I'm releasing you so I can love again."

A tear pierces through and drips off his lashes. The further it falls, the lighter he feels. The tear evaporates. He opens his eyes. "Never forget me. Goodbye, Alexandria."

He leans forward with a humbled smile on his face and lets go.

Number 5, Josh, is dead.

***

Scarlett and I find ourselves embracing each other in front of the window.

Tears stream down my face as I feel stuck in between my imagination and real life.

Scarlett holds back tears of her own. She mumbles, "He needed to let you go. He was attached to you, not you to him. I'm so sorry I rolled my eyes every time you still mention him."

Does she not realize how often she rolls her eyes? If it was a sport, she would be it's Michael Jordan.

I lean my head on her shoulder and snort from chuckling and crying at the same time. "You do that whenever I mention any guy I've dated. And at redheads when they wear polka-dots. And at couples who kiss in grocery stores."

She pets my head. "That's because everyone you date doesn't deserve the air you have to breathe when you speak their name. And grocery stores are for buying food. If I wanted to see people get raunchy over my dinner, I would eat at a strip club."

Tears are still running down my face but I can't stop the smile that is cracking my cheeks. "You have an unhealthy attachment to me and produce."

I often think how strange my life would be without her in it. She has been both the devil on my shoulder and the angel. She is always on board to do whatever and whenever, a true free spirit. I wish I were able to be that light about things. Instead, I create an unhealthy attachment to pretty much everything around me. I have even named my favorite mini skirt and would definitely be upset if I lost or ripped it. I call it Santiago, because for some reason, it's like a magnet for Spanish men.

But Josh also loved me in it. He used to say the green and silver sparkles through the pink fabric reminded him of home. The first time I visited his hometown, I understood why. His family had a farmhouse in Wicklow, just outside Dublin. Gorgeous lakes and the greenest hills and valleys surrounded it. One morning when the sun rose, it hugged the hazy sky and made the clouds glow a pale hue of pink. Not that the atmosphere needed to be any more welcoming, but his sweet, large, and loving family made my stay even more special.

That's the thing with relationships; you not only get connected to the person, but also to their parents and siblings. Then, when things fall apart, you also have to let go of everything that came with it. That sometimes is the hardest part. I allow the entire weight of my head fall onto her shoulder.

Scarlett holds me arms' length away and shakes me until I stop weeping.

The room starts to spin. "Stop it. You're making me dizzy."

She pauses and we look into each other's eyes.

Well, this is awkward. I can tell she doesn't really know what to do next. I smile. "I feel like heterosexual teenagers at a school dance in the 1940s."

She bends her straight arms and pulls me in closer for a tight hug. "If it's wrong, I don't want to be right!"

The stream of tears breaks as my emotions switch to laughter. That sentence is from a comedy we watched a few months ago. Since then, we keep finding perfect moments to use it. This was a good one. She always knows how to make me feel better.

Scarlett runs back to the chairs to grab our glasses off the side table. She spins one hundred and eighty degrees on one foot and walks towards me.

"I think you need some more of this," she states.

I nod in response, maintaining a perfect pout.

I take a large sip of wine and let it sit in my mouth for a second to get a stronger taste of the cabernet grape. Mmm, I sense a hint of vanilla. As I enjoy the deep red liquid flowing into my body, I think of the first time I met Josh. Of course it was where every traditional love story begins—the Santa Anita Park Racetrack.

Scarlett and I were unemployed at the time and looking to make a few quick bucks, so we dressed up wearing the biggest hats we could find in my mother's closet and drove to the horse track. Scarlett caught her reflection in the car window as we arrived and thought she looked ridiculous, so her hat came off. I remember telling her she is going to look out of place as a woman at the racetrack without a big statement piece. I must watch too many movies because no one else was wearing a hat except for me. Probably because there was no royalty in attendance, and it was a Tuesday afternoon. Everyone was staring at me. I was a little embarrassed at first, and then I kind of enjoyed all of the attention, so the hat stayed on.

We watched the post parade then followed the crowd as they headed to the betting counter. While in line, I heard a man say, "nice hat" and I responded with "I would turn to thank you but I'm afraid I'll hit the man behind me with it if I move."

He laughed and said, "I am the man behind you, and you've already hit me twice." I turned around and nearly fainted by how handsome he was.

Throwing my class straight out the window and only thinking with my lower-lady brain, I took him home that same night. The switch to my regular brain mustn't have clicked back because three weeks later, we moved in together.

Scarlett moves her head to try and figure out what I'm staring at. She waves her hand in front of my face. "Earth to Alex!"

I snap out of it.

"Where did you just go?"

I stare out the window. "To a far away land where I realized that, besides my parents' freak of nature successful relationship, moving in with someone after three weeks is not a good idea."

She chuckles sarcastically and with a roll of her eyes she recalls, "Oh, ya. What a hellish ride that relationship was for me. You were up and down, happy and sad, skinny then fat then skinny again."

How dare she! "I was never fat," I offensively reply.

Okay, maybe I gained a little comfortable relationship weight. But don't we all? Sometimes, you get into a groove of working all day then coming home and ordering in. Add a couple glasses of wine while watching some brain numbing reality show until bedtime and boom! Five pounds just appear in the form of love handles and saddle bags.

And, well, it doesn't help that I'm short. An extra few pounds on me and all of a sudden I resemble a tree stump.

I repeat, "I was never fat. Maybe a little soft around the belt-line, but the second I got out of the Josh slump, I toned right back up."

Scarlett shrugs innocently while looking at me through her wine glass. "Ya, staying with Josh that long was a mistake, you should have left at the first sign of cellulite."

I quickly look behind me at my hamstrings. I sigh. Good, all clear. That silly bitch is just trying to get a rise out of me.

She laughs. "Just kidding. But the Irishman did last longer than he should with the way he treated you at the end."

She wasn't wrong. He was so unhappy with himself, and the longer I stuck around, the more he took his own shitty feelings out on me. I distinctively remember being called a "caffler" too often.

But she wasn't one to talk about keeping mistakes around too long. Let me jog her memory.

"If I remember correctly, a week after I moved in with Josh, you upped and left to Indonesia where you met a local man. Who was backpacking. In his own country. Then brought him back to the states and let him stay with you. For a year."

"We were in love!" Scarlett shouts defensively.

How deluded could she be? "He was a homeless man! Who didn't even speak English!"

She waves my points away. "Pff! Who needs to communicate, anyways?"

Yep. Completely delusional. Hasn't she read any articles on how to make a relationship last? Every old couple always has the same thing to say, *communication*. Without that, you may as well be dating a mannequin. I lift my arm in the air, hoping to be heard this time. "Regular people, that's who."

She brings my arm down and before taking another sip of her soul soother she recalls, "I taught him to say *I'm horny* and *looks nice*. I tried to get him to say *you look sexy*, but it was too hard for him to pronounce".

I giggle a little. She is one unique chick. I could never date someone I couldn't talk to. I'd have a vacation fling with him, but never bring him home for good. It would drive me crazy. The guitar playing until all hours of the night and his low hygiene standard would just send me right over the edge. Though, I guess sometimes silence is overrated. I share. "Well, in comparison, Josh and I may have lasted longer if we spoke less. Correction. Yelled less".

Scarlett walks back to the chair, takes a seat, crosses her legs, and fills up her already half-full wine glass.

I do the same. Why not? There is more of the night to come, and I can't let her enjoy this delicious *sauvignon rouge* on her own. What kind of a friend would that make me? We're on this ride together and I have a feeling it may be getting a little bumpier ahead.

With two mouthfuls and a deep breath later, I take a more serious tone.

"Josh and I were together for three years. Our love was intense and comfortable at the same time. We fought, bickered, argued, yelled at the top of our lungs, threw things, stormed out, and came back then made love as if it was our last day on Earth. At the end of the night, no matter what happened, we lusted after each other unconditionally. I mean, loved." No, I mean, lusted.

Scarlett laughs. "He's Irish and you're American, but you guys sound like a couple of Columbians."

I guess it doesn't take a Latin background to have a fiery connection. Ours was a mix of fire and ice, though. "He was close with my family and I his. We bought a condo in LA and he was completely convinced we would get married and grow old together." Well, I bought the condo. He was still trying to get noticed by UEFA and refused to get any help from my father's connections. Typical stubborn guy. Though my dad actually respected him for that.

I continue, "We were a family—a dysfunctional, toxic, and unhealthy family, but one nonetheless."

She points in the air. "*Toxic* being the key word".

She doesn't have to chime in with her judging comments every time I finish a sentence. I give her a look expressing that. She seems to get it, as she doesn't respond, so I continue.

"But I wasn't happy with the roller coaster motion. I hated walking on eggshells to avoid a fight. I hated not being able to watch football. I hated having to hide my past from him so he didn't feel insecure or jealous. I hated that he hated strawberries. I hated never being able to joke about wanting to squeeze a strange man's butt without him accusing me of wanting to sleep with the guy."

Scarlett lifts her hand, interrupting me. "Well, that last one is not normal, Alex."

So she is suddenly an expert on normal? This coming from the woman who just admitted the two most important words to teach a foreign person is *horny* and *pretty*. So what, I like to look at hot guys—it's completely innocent. The man I end up with is going to have to embrace the fact that I am a people watcher, and sure, those people just happen to have buns of steel. I'm sure I'll find someone who understands. Or maybe just doesn't notice. Ya, that's more likely.

"The point is that I hated who I had to be for him. It took me three years, but I realized that being with Josh meant I wasn't able to be myself."

I feel my chest become tighter as I get a little angry. How dare he want me to be a different person? I am super awesome. I've met the freakin Queen of England! Sure, I was four years old, and it was because my father won his second Grand Prix and was invited to a fancy gala she happened to also attend. But still. I huff then take a calming sip.

Mmm mmm, ya, that feels better.

Scarlett shakes her head. "No woman should have to change who they are for a man. And if a man doesn't love you just the way you are, he can hit the fucking road, Jack."

I nod in agreement, already having gone through anger and acceptance in my mind before her comment.

"The more he fell in love with me, the worse he got. It was so frustrating. I was unhappy so one day I let him know, asked him to move out, and left to open the store early. For the next year, he worked on fixing himself so he could get me back. That never happened."

Sometimes, a girl makes up her mind and there is no possible way a man can change it. That's what happened with me. I knew I didn't want to be around his kind of negativity and if I was ever caught missing him, I just reminded myself of that fact. It was a simple mantra. Scar was really supportive during that time, and was a huge part of why it was so easy to move on from him.

She lifts her head up, matter of factly. "He wasn't *the one* and I think you knew that for quite a bit of time. After you left him, you changed back into yourself within minutes. It was the best decision you've ever made."

Well, I couldn't disagree. She can be hard on the guys I am with, but in this case, she was right not to approve.

"I truly did love him but I'm not sure he loved himself. Leaving him made me feel like I had one less thing to worry about. I think I released my attachment to him a long time ago, but I needed him to let *me* go. And now that he has, I feel, once again, like I have one less thing to worry about. In fact, my heart suddenly feels a little healthier."

I couldn't be his crutch anymore. He needed to realize that heartbreak is a part of being human. That he can heal and find love again. It's a big world. He is making a name for himself in the UEFA circuit and will no doubt find a hot little bunny soon.

I do hope he starts loving himself first, though, or history will probably repeat itself. But it's not my problem anymore, is it?

The image of Josh fades from my memory. *Goodbye, Josh.*

And just like that, he is gone. A smile creases my cheeks and I take a breezy breath in. Oh, that feels good.

"I'm proud of him. And you." Scar leans over and brushes off my shoulder. "On to the next one."

How sweet does that sound! Not her rap, but the thought of being done with Josh. That was a heavy one. I feel like dancing. A really happy hop bounces through my body.

"On to the next one."

Chapter Twenty-Two

It's A Duel!

Clint stares at the ledge that used to have Josh standing on it.

Both get startled when they hear the sniper's shot. *Bang!* Confirming Josh's demise.

Matteo maintains a calm and composed demeanor.

Clint waits a few seconds then shakes his head. "I'm confused."

Matteo turns to face Clint. "Why? A man realizing he was holding back the one he loved from finding love is confusing to you? Have you ever been in love?"

Clint is surprised at what he felt was an insulting comment but responds without being defensive. "I've loved—"

Matteo interrupts, gesturing his hands side to side. "Let me guess, you've loved things, but not people?"

Clint raises his hands up in defense and walks closer to him. "Hey man, I'm not like Rob or Josh. I don't get personal with strangers."

Matteo puffs his chest out and takes a step towards Clint, proving he doesn't intimidate him. "We are the last two men up here. We can either talk it out or fight it out. Your choice."

Clint raises his brow. "Talk or fight what out?"

Matteo takes another step forward and points at Cliff with his hand cocked sideways and shaped like a gun. "Your issues. Or would you prefer to die without your soul being cleared of all blocks?"

Clint walks away, turning his back to Matteo. Frustration builds up inside his heart and mind. No one tells him what to do.

"My soul? Die? Enough with the preaching, Wise Man Matteo. That shit doesn't work on me. Don't forget I am still here." He heavily pounds his chest with a folded fist. "I could kill you right now and not have to answer any bullshit questions."

Matteo leans his head to the side, pouts his lip, and patronizingly pushes Clint's buttons. "Oh, so you have father-son issues. Did he not love you? Did you even know him?"

Clint scrunches his face with irritation. "No, you're wrong. My dad and I are close."

Matteo lifts his hand in the air and quickly replies before Clint could continue his sentence. "Aha. A personal response. There is a real human being inside that expensive suit."

Clint rolls his eyes and shakes his head. He realizes Matteo is playing a game. He doesn't respond. He picks up the axe from the floor, throws it over his shoulder, turns around, and walks to the bar.

Matteo follows curiously with a smile so mischievous, you can almost see it curling at both ends.

Clint looks for the Gran Patrón Platinum he noticed earlier and sees it under the bar next to Sebastian's corpse. He contemplates whether or not the prized Tequila is worth having to touch a dead body. After a very short pause, he decides it is.

Without any care or remorse, Matteo steps over Alec and pushes Henry's body over to make room for a place to sit. He picks up the stool from off the floor, brushes the wet blood off the seat, and watches Clint with a predatory gaze.

Clint reaches for the expensive bottle, grazing Sebastian's pant, and makes a revolted grunt. He slowly opens the lid while looking for a glass that doesn't have blood spattered all over it. He finds one and while pouring a more than generous amount, he addresses Matteo. "I know what you are trying to do."

Matteo leans on a tightened fist and answers with a smug look on his face. "And what is that?"

Clint takes a small sip of his favorite liquor. "It's an amateur trick. Try and break down your opponent mentally so you gain the advantage."

Matteo raises a brow, intrigued by his speculation.

Clint continues. "You can't play mind games with me and expect to win. What you can expect..." he takes another sip of the world famous Tequila and swallows really loudly,

"...is that I will always do whatever it takes to win."

Matteo sits up straight and smugly grins again. He realizes Clint is more than a lost cause and defense preparation may be necessary. He gets off the stool and calmly walks towards the balcony where Josh met his end.

Clint shouts with an ultra deep tone, "Where do you think you're going?"

Matteo pauses and can almost hear the testosterone building inside Clint. He decides not to entertain the question and continues to walk.

One step later, Matteo jerks forward as a glass shatters on the back of his head. Hurt but not injured, he shakes it off and turns around to face Clint.

Clint stands proud. He grips one of the bloody glasses and aims at the arrogant grin staring back.

Matteo moves aside. He looks down and laughs. "Miss."

Clint throws another.

Matteo ducks. "Miss, again."
Clint huffs with anger.

Matteo takes a few steps backwards, arriving at Liam's corpse.

Clint scrambles behind the bar looking for something heavier. He throws a bottle.

Smash! The Belvedere Vodka echoes as it breaks below Matteo's feet.

Clint reaches over to the shelf and slings the rest of the glasses in the air. So enraged, he barely aims.

Matteo gets angrier and angrier as he finds it more difficult to avoid the thrown objects. The blackness of the sky plays tricks on his mind.

Clint throws the Patrón, aiming this time.

Contact. A sharp pain pierces through Matteo's leg. He looks down and sees glass sticking through his pant. He makes a grunting sound as he pulls the jagged, blood-soaked shard out of his flesh.

Clint arrogantly shouts at Matteo, "And the hunter now becomes the prey! How poetic."

Matteo squats down and pulls the arrow out of Liam's body. He looks for where he placed the bow. He sees it a few paces away on the floor. He stays low and moves towards it.

Crash! Another bottle smashes next to him on the floor. He frowns at the thought of Clint's relentlessness and then smiles as he is actually a little impressed. He places the arrow to the bow, stands up straight, lifts it up to his chin, takes a deep breath in and thinks, *it is going to feel so sweet to end this prick's life. Sweet like limoncello.*

Clint turns around to grab the last bottle off the shelf.

Matteo struggles to focus clearly through the darkness. He sees Clint's figure move and he waits until he stands still.

Clint turns around and lifts his arm back, preparing to launch the inebriant.

Matteo sees his chance and takes it. He releases the arrow on an exhale and feels the adrenaline flow through his lungs on the following inhale.

As the arrow flies through the air, Clint jerks his body to the right as he throws the bottle with all of his might.

The arrow enters his left shoulder.

Clint gets thrown back, hits the glass shelf with force, and watches as it collapses down on him.

Matteo charges forward, avoiding the bottle, and arrives at the bar to see the result of his shot.

Clint immediately rises to his feet through the pile of broken glass with cuts all over his body and faces Matteo inches away.

Matteo notices his missed shot in Clint's shoulder. He looks down at Clint's arm and his heart sinks to his feet.

Holding the axe in his hand, Clint raises it above his head.

Matteo reaches into his back pocket, then steps into Clint.

The two bloodied men stand body to body.

A second passes and the axe falls to the ground behind Clint's back.

Matteo holds his pocketknife in Clint's abdomen. He clenches the handle tight and raises the knife upwards to go through more of Clint's organs.

Clint stands for the last time, shocked. He looks at Matteo and realizes there is no escape, except embracing the inevitable. Death.

The light of his existence goes black. He can't see, hear, or even think anymore.

Clint, Number 10, is dead.

Chapter Twenty-Three

Age Is Just A Number

Holy shit, that was a thrill!

My shoes are off, my palms are all sweaty, and I find myself sitting on my knees on the chaise longue.

I'm glad Clint put up a little bit of a fight. He was a killer in the courtroom, so I know he had it in him. If I were on that rooftop, I'd also probably use the glass-throwing angle. Something about smashing things is so liberating. Though, I guess if it were a life or death situation, using the axe Viking style straight away would be more effective. This Hollywood hot shot was far from a fierce warrior, but I did enjoy the battle. This time, my heart doesn't race with adrenaline but instead, with anticipation and excitement. I bounce up and down like a monkey.

Scarlett starts clapping. "What a momentous achievement!"

I join her in the clapping parade. Clapping makes me feel like I've won something. I suppose I did. "I know! Ugh! I am so done with him!"

She stops clapping at once. "As you know, I never liked that guy. What a douche bag he was."

I laugh and joke, "Who did you like?"

Scarlett ignores my comment, waving her hand in the air. "I was so proud of you for being in control during that relationship and ending it before it got serious."

My legs start to feel cold, as I'm pretty sure they aren't getting proper circulation. I lift up off my knees and stretch them out. "I knew his type. He saw something he wanted, and he got it. I figured I had to be in control from day one, and to do that, I needed him to chase me for some time."

Scarlett smiles and shakes her head. "So dating Clint was just a game? See if you could be the woman to settle the player down? Classic chick mistake. When will our gender ever learn?"

It's true. I loved our little cat and mouse charade. It was like an extracurricular activity—something super fun to do in my spare time. No harm, no foul, right?

But it wasn't for the game; it was to keep the romance alive. I shrug in defense.

"I wasn't trying to change him. I was trying to see if we could work as a couple."

As women, we kind of get-off being desired. Sure, it sounds narcissistic but as soon as we are no longer feeling desirable, our vaginas dry up and we turn into real bitches. The best advice I can give to a man is to never stop chasing your girl around the house, the yard, the town, and the whole freaking country if necessary. The second you stop is when she starts thinking about looking elsewhere for someone who may want her more.

Scarlett spills some wine on her arm and licks it up, then points at me. "Lies! He was determined to crack you but you weren't ever really truly convinced about him."

Should I address the fact that she just acted exactly like a cat? I guess it is expensive juice. I'd probably have done the same thing. I nod. "I always kept him at a safe distance emotionally because I knew he wasn't the one. He had everything going for him but was still not settled with himself. He had never been married, engaged, or even lived with anyone. Red flags galore."

She raises a brow with confusion written all over her face. "So why were you still attached to him?"

I answer honestly. "I am twenty-eight. He is intelligent, handsome, and playful. I thought he would have been a great dad."

I was a little embarrassed to say that out loud. Did I really just admit that I was now looking for a mate based on his potential parental qualities? I mean, I don't want a sperm donor. I want love. What was I thinking?

Scarlett almost knocks over her glass of wine as she throws her hands in the air. "This was about your womb?"

She and I are the same age, coming very close to that scary three and zero. She must have thought about a potential baby daddy once or twice.

I give her a death stare and then smooth out my frown lines in between my eyebrows.

"I've put so much pressure on myself to have the societal norm of a life plan. You know, university degree first, good job second, get married in your mid-late twenties third, and have a baby or babies before thirty."

Scarlett swivels her head around like a guest on Jerry Springer. "So you were just going to settle for him because it was the socially acceptable timeline to do so? No. You aren't a normal chick, Alex."

What was that supposed to mean? Am I different because of the life I grew up in, or because I have a huge Quasimodo lump growing out of my back that no one has told me about? All right, so that's highly unlikely, I guess she just means I'm unique. Yep. That's what I'm going with. I'll take it as a compliment then. I lift my head up.

"Thank you."

She nods. "Clint was successful and handsome and older, but he was so concerned with everything being perfect that he may never be truly happy in a relationship. That is not the life you want to be a part of."

I tilt my head in agreement then take a large sip of the burgundy elixir.

Despite knowing from the beginning that he wasn't the one, we still made a good time out of it. Probably because we always had so much fun together, but I knew it had to come to an end sooner or later. The standard three months passed and I asked him one day if he was happier with me in his life than without. He paused. Then he said yes. I told him I am looking for a "no question about it" kind of love, and this was just not it. He didn't disagree. And not that it will come to a surprise to anyone, but he is still single.

While I have a moment inside my brain, Scarlett sees an opportunity to complain.

"This is the frustrating thing with getting older; they tell you that you have to know exactly what you want in order to get it. But as more and more people don't end up being what you want, you end up getting too comfortable with your independent way of living. Soon 'exactly what you want' becomes impossible to find. And before you know it, you're fifty, alone, and empty. This is the future Clint would see if he looked into a magic crystal ball. You have to accept that there is nothing you can do to save it."

Really? She can't possibly believe in fortunetellers. Well, maybe she does. We did get our palms read from a gypsy in Turkey once. She told me I would have five sons and that Scar would meet the love of her life near water. I hope that's not why Scar keeps investing in vacation flings. The world is covered in water; it's like the lady wasn't even trying.

I roll my eyes. "How dramatic. Everyone who gets older realizes that all they want is a lover and friend they can breed with."

Scarlett takes a dramatic breath in, thinks for a second and responds, "Ya, that's true. But still, Clint is a douche. Let the wind take that one far away. You will have the life you want and he won't be a part of it. That is my final comment about him."

I smile. When your job is basically receiving lavish gifts from sorry snobby socialites for making their DUI's go away as fast as possible, you may become a little douchey. You can't really avoid that title when you have eleven Lamborghinis—one in every color. Yes, even pink.

I shrug. "You're right. I know there is a really cool guy out there that I can high five and make babies with. Definitely one who loves me more than his haircut."

I chuckle then shake my head. "It's not Clint and I am okay with that."

From this moment forward, I am going to throw my stereotypical timeline out the window and start living day to day. I still want that special kind of love, but settling isn't an option, so I will wait until it shows up at my front door. That's how it always happens, right? But please don't be the guy who delivers our Thai, he's far too hairy. I giggle.

Scarlett looks at me with squinted eyes and on a long exhale asks, "So what are we going to do about Matteo?"

Chapter Twenty-Four

The Last Man Standing

Matteo feels the soul escape from Clint's shell. Holding onto his knife, he lets the body fall to the ground, collapsing on top of Sebastian.

He comprehends the reality of the situation and takes three large steps backwards.

This is it. I won. This is my second chance.

Matteo walks around the room and takes it all in. He wonders if he should move the bodies or leave them how they are.

He decides to leave them.

Chad's body is remembered by the wire that still hangs over the ledge.

Tommy's corpse lies over a pot light near the middle of the room. A red glow beams through the drained life source.

The shell of football star, Alec, remains limp over a fallen stool.

Henry's long figure resembles a fallen-down tree as he is straight and stiff in front of the bar, next to Alec.

Rob's chiseled features are unrecognizable, covered in blood, folded on the floor next to Henry.

Sebastian's muscular physique is covered in broken glass and spilled booze behind the bar.

A hole is visible through Liam's chest where the arrow took his life near the ledge.

Josh's body remains unseen.

Clint's face kisses the shattered shelf on the concrete floor, draped over Sebastian.

Feeling proud and worthy to be the last man standing, Matteo puffs his chest and lifts his hands high in the air. He lets out a celebratory "Woohoo."

He pauses as he hears noise coming from somewhere. He tosses his vision around the room but can't see anything. He forms a defensive stance with his legs wide, knees bent, and fists forward.

I open the steel door and walk out onto the rooftop. My white dress makes Matteo think of an angel.

I gasp a little when I see the rage has not yet left his eyes. It actually frightens me. His disheveled hair and ripped clothes makes it look like he's been on a deserted island for months. He is still bleeding from the glass wound and his fists remain clenched.

He releases his grip and reaches his arms out in my direction.

"I'm sorry." His voice trembles with emotion.

With all that adrenaline rushing through his veins, I half expected him to be charging at me like a wild bull. I'm glad he isn't, but it's not yet time for feelings. I have to take charge.

Trying to keep all the emotions out of my voice, I gesture towards him. "Congratulations, you are the last man breathing."

He walks forward with caution. "So what happens now, Alexandria?"

I find it extremely difficult to look at him. Not only because he is covered in blood, but also because it's become second nature for me to avoid him since our split.

He softens his voice. "I realized after Josh let go that I would be standing here, in front of you. Face to face. Like I have been wishing for over three years."

The pot lights shine through me as I walk nervously closer to Matteo. I slip a little as I pass Tommy but catch my balance immediately. Close one. I do not want to get blood on this Hervé Léger. I sweep my hair behind my shoulders, reclaiming my composure.

"And how did you know that? Clint had an axe. That is a serious weapon. He could have been an expert at axe throwing for all you knew." I smirk.

Matteo knows I tend to hide my nerves through humor. One thing he always had a knack for was seeing through people's bullshit. Almost as if he could read body language. Rare for a carpenter.

He does not react. He steps closer and closer to me until the realm of my personal space is invaded. I can almost feel his breath on my skin.

Whoa. This is far too close. I push my hands out and step back.

His posture relaxes and I look up to see a tear slowly stream down his face. He ignores my request and takes a step forward, then gently grips my waist.

He is relentless. But when I allow myself to feel his strong hands wrapped around my hips, I become blind to all of the death and destruction around us. Each body disappears. We become the only two people in the room. A sense of safety and comfort hugs my insides, which is always how I felt around him.

He leans into me and tucks my hair behind my ears. This time, it didn't bother me.

He whispers, "I knew you wouldn't be able to let me go without having the courage to forgive me."

Why does my body feel like stars are dancing on my skin? Every touch and feeling is heightened. I close my eyes while my nerves intensify and say honestly, "I am facing you right now, but I still don't feel like I have the courage to forgive you."

Matteo tries to look into my eyes but I can't bring myself to open them yet. He grazes my face with the back of his hand. "I'm sorry."

There's that word again. It's said so often that I don't hold meaning to it anymore. I take his hand off my face, turn my head away, and say with built up bitterness, "That's not enough. It has never been enough."

Matteo reaches out for my shoulder, refusing to let me walk away. He looks down to the floor. "There is no love stronger than a mother's love…" He raises his gaze to me. "…And there is no hate stronger than a mother's hate."

My head swivels up to face his. The nerves feel like they are eating away at the pit of my stomach. What does he know about maternal desire? Nothing. My lip curls up as my resentment hits an all-time high.

Matteo sees he's pinched a nerve with me. He recalls the first day we met at a café in Rome and tries to calm me down by repeating the first words he ever said to me.

"I can tell you're a special woman. I can see there is a fire in your eyes, and I would like to be with you for the rest of my life."

The angry thoughts melt away and my knees buckle a little, just like they did that sunny afternoon. The café was called Corviva. Scar and I were waiting for our friend Ivey to arrive before heading down to wine country. I nearly spat out my espresso when a handsome local knelt down beside our table in the pose of a proposal. Normally, I wouldn't have fallen for such cheesiness, but there was something different about him. It was his eyes. They ate me up. He looked at me and the entire world ceased to exist.

He ended up coming along with us to Tuscany. The girls loved him, too. He and Scar spoke Italian together and Ivey was ecstatic to be taken to the best spots only locals knew about. There wasn't a person he ever met that didn't like him. He could have had any girl he wanted, but he didn't care, he only saw me, and that of course made me weak in the knees.

We had a fire between us that neither of us could deny. We knew we were too different for a relationship to ever work, but we could never be in the same room without being all over each other. We hardly ever said, "How was your day?" before my legs were around his waist and our tongues were in each other's mouths.

So when we found out I was pregnant, it wasn't exactly a shock to either of us.

My chin starts to curl as tears build up in my eyes and I reply the same words I did that first day.

"If you think you can handle my fire, I should stay away from you."

We both smile.

Matteo embraces me and places his soft lips on mine.

Oh, how wonderful it feels to kiss him again. He is like a drug. That's exactly what he is to me. I can't let his pillowy touch distract me. I push him off.

"This is why I haven't seen you, Matteo. I can't think clearly when you're around."

Matteo smiles so wide it verges on smug. "Alexandria, you choose to block out your thoughts when you're around me because you're afraid of feeling the pain you did before."

He always does this. Delve into people's psyches without permission. He works with goddamn wood for a living! He's nearly the furthest thing from a psychiatrist. He should stay out of my head.

As I deeply inhale, the buried emotions start to flow in. No matter how frustrating he can be, the jerk is right. I turn around and let the tears gush out without wiping them away. "I didn't have to feel that pain, Matteo! You made me!"

I turn back and see his burly hands covering his face.

His voice is muffled through his palms. "I'm sorry. I didn't know what I be would losing."

Ugh. So what? Now he expects to receive sympathy because he only realized what he had when he lost it? Typical.

I frustratingly tear his hands away from his face. "When I found out I was pregnant, I was so happy. And I thought you'd feel the same way. You were so in love with me. The last thing I expected was for you to make me feel like I wasn't good enough to be a mother."

He leans closer to me.

I step back.

No. I'm putting up my invisible shield. I won't let him distract me with his smooth tanned skin, strong brawny shoulders, and perfectly shaped lips. I shake my head attempting to snap out of it. Now that he's re-opened the wound in my heart, all I really feel for him now is hate.

He holds out his hands, pleading. "Alexandria, we knew each other for four months. Sure, I already knew I loved you, but I was scared. It's not how I saw my life play out."

Yes, he prays and preaches, but that doesn't make him God. The biggest problem with Matteo was that he was a man of no compromise. He spent a lot of time coming to the distinction of what was right and wrong and when he did, it was set in stone.

When we found out about the pregnancy, his first reaction was, *Well, we can't keep it.* I was so overcome with anger I could have actually killed him right then and there.

But instead, I shut off my emotional switch and went completely cold. Frozen enough to practically stop caring all together. I thought if that is how he felt then he mustn't be *the one*, so there was no point keeping him around. That afternoon, I left him.

Tears bubble through what feels like every part of my being. My lungs fill with sorrow and I have trouble gasping for air. I pound my fist to my chest.

"My heart broke when you told me we shouldn't have the baby. I knew it wasn't the right time and logically it made sense to terminate because to you, it was just a seed and not a baby." I throw my hands in the air. "And who cares if they kill a seed, right?"

I could hear myself starting to sound irrational. That's what happens when my emotions take over.

I bring my hands down to my heart. "You may have thought like that, but I didn't. I couldn't help but feel connected to this seed inside of me. I couldn't help but feel like I was contemplating ending a life. A life we made together."

I struggle to take enough of an inhale to be able to raise my voice. "You treated it as if it was a stock option. 'It's not the right time to invest, maybe in a few more years'. When I heard that, I couldn't believe it was coming from your mouth." I poke my finger to his chest. "From you. The guy who said the Archangels of light, love, and security brought me to you. Where was science in that statement?"

Matteo holds my hand. "Having a child out of wedlock is so far from traditional and I was worried how everyone, especially my family, would perceive it. But losing you was worse than having a few family members upset."

Well, he got that right. Opening up this floodgate overwhelms me with the sense of guilt. It wrenches my gut. The only reason I was able to go about my day with a smile on my face was because I blocked Matteo out of my mind. As soon as a thought crept in, I would occupy my brain with designers, new fabrics, sensational wine, and good company.

It worked really well until right now. Ugh, talking to him is making this worse. I'm pretty sure there is steam piping out my ears.

"So let me get this straight. A bastard child is not acceptable, but an abortion is?

He holds my hand tighter and tilts his head trying to get through to me. "I felt conflicted with the thought of playing God, I did. I do admit that my judgment was obstructed by my current and past relatives' stance on unwed mothers. I prayed and prayed. I even went to see Father Augustus who understood my inner battle. He gave me absolution for my sins."

He did not just say that. Well, I'm glad his conscience is cleared. I guess we are all done, then. We can wipe our hands off and go home to watch a re-run of Seinfeld. Even in my thoughts, I'm sarcastic, but we'll leave that problem for another day.

I push my fist to his chest.

"I'm glad it was so easy for you to forget."

"Forgive, not forget, Alexandria." He pulls my hand to his face and kisses it.

My eyes roll.

He places my hand back on his chest. "But before that, trust me, my soul was in pain. The thing that hurt me the most was that you wouldn't let me help you through it. I was a part of it, too. I wanted to be with you throughout the process."

I stop crying and just get angry. "You wanted to go through the process with me? Well, this is how it went. I showed up at the clinic. They put an incredibly painful tent in my vagina, then I got sent to another clinic where I had to sit with ten other women who wouldn't stop saying the words *fetus* and *abortion*."

I take a deep breath in and can almost see fire gust out as I exhale. "Then I went into a surgical room where they injected a heavy dose of anesthesia and scooped out the baby, sorry, seed…" I correct myself while sarcastically holding up quotation signs. I huff, then continue. "…And all while I was asleep. I woke up thirty minutes later with a diaper on and blood everywhere. Then I bled and cried and bled and cried for the next three weeks."

Matteo wraps his arms around me and cries. His embrace helps regulate my racing heartbeat. Is it bad that hearing him weep is making me feel better? I have never seen him cry before. I always thought he was too proud to cry. It felt healing, for the both of us, to have him let his emotions go, even if he is probably drooling on my dress.

Matteo's body bounces from his uncontrollable sobbing. "I'm so sorry. I'm so sorry. Please forgive me. I never wanted to be a father. I know I was being selfish. I will never hurt you again."

I wipe my tears away then push him back to face me. Suddenly, I can look into his eyes and feel nothing. Could his mesmerizing hold of me finally be gone? I smooth my hand over my chest and sense my heart filling up.

"I really needed to hear that, Matteo."

Through pouting lips, he manages to defend himself. "I've said it a thousand times before."

I smile and cup his face in my hand. "I know, but now I am ready."

Matteo looks at me with uncertainty in his gaze. "Ready for what?"

I close my eyes as the last tear sneaks its way out. "Ready to forgive you. Going through what we did is not something I would ever wish upon my worst enemy, but you're right."

He sniffles and lifts his brows in shock. "I'm right?"

I smile. "Yes. I was twenty-five and hormonal and blamed it all on you. But the truth is, I wasn't ready to be a mother. It wasn't my time. And maybe that seed wasn't ready to be a human. I know my chance to have a little one will come again. And I will be the most loving mother it could ever hope for."

Matteo dries his tears and smiles at me with respect and admiration. "I knew you were a special woman. I still want to spend the rest of my life with you."

Ha. Well, there is no shot of that happening. Fool me once—you know how the rest goes. Though, I think it is sweet that he still believes in us. It's a sign that couples really could get through this time if they stick together.

But since I ran like a bat out of hell, our chances of lasting are long gone. If I had the power to change things, I may have, but I don't have a time machine. The only thing I can do now is move forward fearlessly with an open mind and an unattached heart.

I hold his face. "No, Matteo, you aren't *the one*. I'm grateful for the life lessons you have taught me because they've made me a stronger woman. You've made me a stronger woman."

Matteo stares back into my eyes with a worried look.

I smooth the back of my hand on his soft olive skin one last time. "Thank you, Matteo."

Scarlett slowly sneaks up behind me and hands me a knife.

I don't take it.

I close my eyes, breathe deeply, and let go all of my emotional attachments to Matteo.

Scarlett moves me to the side and thrusts the knife into Matteo's torso. She needed to release a little bit of her negative connection to him for what he made me go through. She stood by my side the entire way, just as she did tonight. Her anger towards him dies, along with his body.

A smile stretches across my face and kisses my cheeks as his essence begins to disappear. I open my eyes and he is gone.

Matteo, Number 7, is dead.

***

Scarlett and I stand on the rooftop lounge of the Theodore hotel. All ten of my exes are gone.

My heart, mind, and soul have been cleared of all bitterness, resentment, rejection, insecurity, anger, shame, guilt, love, lust, and loss. Yet, I feel more whole than I ever have.

The dawn begins to break and the warmth of the summer sun dances on our skin.

I take Scarlett's hand, look at her, and smile. *Thank you,* I say with a flicker of my lashes.

She nods and smiles back, holding her head up showing how proud she is.

I release my grip when I turn around in my pale platform heels and wiggle to adjust the super-tight Hervé Léger mini dress.

My dark brown hair waves over my shoulder in the morning breeze. I purse my glossed lips and blink my smoky blue eyes.

I pause before I exit through the metal rooftop door to look back.

Eight lounge chairs reappear with new names on them.

My head quickly swivels to Scarlett as I happily announce, "Your turn."

Here's a sneak peek into the next *Exes* adventure by Jerrica Zeron

Axing *Her* Exes

"Puuussshhh!" Scarlett obnoxiously screams at my belly before nonchalantly wrapping her lips around a flask of vodka.

Does she think yelling is going to induce this labour? I know she desperately wants her drinking partner back, but I'm still two weeks away from my due date. She'll just have to wait–preferably in silence. I reach my head to peek around the corner into the foyer to shout, "Blanca, can you please tell this crazy bitch to stop screaming at my unborn baby? It must be bad for it or something, right?"

I keep my gaze steady until my flustered Colombian midwife slides on the marble tile, stopping in the centre of the entrance to my sunroom. Man, she looks like a sweaty mess. What was she doing back there?

We both stare as she regains her breath. She pats her forehead dry then shakes her pointed finger at Scarlett.

"Shut your big mouth!" she scolds using a thicker-than-usual Spanish accent.

Whoa. Easy there, Blanca. No need to swallow her head whole. I just wanted you to suggest the volume lower, not encourage her to take out her hoops and raise the temperature in here to *ghetto*. I can feel my eyes blink, anxiously awaiting my feisty friend's reaction.

Scar's back immediately straightens and her eye starts to twitch with rage.

I turn to her and burst out in laughter. "Ha. Big mouth. Best."

They both ignore my existence. I switch my gaze from one Latina to the other. They seem to be having some sort of stare-off. I don't know if it's hormones or the heated air they're generating, but I am suddenly craving gelato. No. A spicy burrito. No. Both.

Scarlett tightens her lips like an angry grandma. She rests her flask on the couch and uncrosses her legs, getting ready to stand up and charge.

Yep. Just as I thought–she's overreacting. Shocker. I reach out and grab her shirt, pulling her back into the plush leather sofa.

She folds her arms and huffs into her chest.

I send a smile towards the uncensored South American. "Thank you, Blanca. That was glorious." And a little harsh, I suppose. I should probably tell her to take smaller bites next time. Oh, that reminds me! "Would you be a peach and get us something to snack on? Something cold. And something hot. That would be lovely."

Blanca reluctantly nods and spins around in her socks.

Oh, and I forgot to ask for something to drink. I raise my hand in the air. "And a water with lemon." *Head shake*. "No, sorry. Lemonade would be better."

She turns back and shoots me a look that basically screams, *this isn't my job*.

Hmm. She's right. Though, if I make it pregnancy-related, it will be. "With some sugar on the side." I rub my belly. "The baby loves sugar".

Awesome save. God, I'm really gonna miss blaming everything on this kid when it pops out.

As soon as she disappears into the hallway, Scar looks at me with squinted eyes and a clenched jaw.

"That bitch is asking to get cut. You know that, right?"

I playfully punch her shoulder. "Ha. Scarlett, she's nearly sixty years old. Leave bitter Blanca alone."

Scar smiles with approval of the new nickname.

Damnit. The second I said it I knew it would stick. Woops. I shrug. Maybe she'll forget if I change the subject back to her exes. Worth a try. I scooch closer to her. "So they're on a deserted island and Alejandro just fell off a tree while trying to get coconuts."

An unlikely scenario considering he was an experienced climber, but I'll let it go. It took me almost three years to convince her to participate in this exercise, so tonight is her night to be in control.

I gesture for her to continue.

She interlaces her fingers and gently places them on her lap. "Yes, we're three down. Five more to go." She looks up to the ceiling, closing her eyes against the rays streaming through the skylight.

"The men rush towards the fallen fruit, ignoring the body they're surrounding. The blistering sun pierces their skin and they become closer to dehydration by the minute. Lucas cracks the coconut against the tree and lifts it above his head, letting the liquid fall onto his plump lips–"

Shit. I have to pee again. I raise my hand. "Hold that thought, be right back."

With many thanks to Mom and Dad for teaching me that a solid family unit can get each other through anything. We're f-ing Zeron's. To my non-reader busy as hell sister, Jen, for giving me her feedback on multiple rounds of this story, accusing me for writing about every girls night she's ever had. To my sister Jade for letting me exploit her bangin body on the cover, and for cheering me on every step of the way. To my brother Scott for trying to teach me that vulgarity isn't always the best policy. I'm sorry it still hasn't sunk in. To my best friend, Melissa, for, well, proving what 'best' really means. Thank you for being the backboard to every ping pong idea and encouraging me to always jump into the deep-end headfirst. You are my muse. To my fiancé, Johan, for giving me the opportunity to live out my life's dream of becoming an author. You are the only reason I haven't gone absolutely mad during this process. When I start to lose it, your ridiculous dance moves never fail to make me laugh. Älskar dig. To Ingela and Janne for your support and for reminding me to eat and get fresh air during the lockdown days of my first draft. To Sara Sepehri for her invaluable creative support, marketing assistance and for making me believe in her crazy idea—that I could actually be a smashing success. Line it up! To Xarvan Khavari for taking my idea and bringing it to life through your amazing graphic designing skills. To my editor Zee Monodee for more things than I can name on one page. Your publishing knowledge and expertise has taught me more than I could have ever imagined. Without you, this would have ended up being an eighty page movie script. You are amazing! Finally, to all my family, friends, editors and cover designers, my dedicated blogger followers and everyone involved in this process—Thank you for embracing and accepting my quirky, sometimes controlling, and mostly inappropriate behaviour. High-five.

About The Author

Jerrica Zeron is a mid-twenty sarcastic and stylish unfiltered storyteller. She received her first writing award at the age of eleven and hasn't stopped scribbling her quirky thoughts onto paper ever since. She was born in Montreal, Quebec and raised in Oakville, Ontario. Her extremely close-knit family is comprised of all freak-of-nature-talented individuals whom inspire most of her ideas. She worked in the hustle and bustle of politics before meeting her Swedish fiancé on the beaches of Aruba one crazy New Years Eve night. Sixteen months later she moved to Sweden and began her career as an author. She loves cooking, traveling and taking risks every chance she can. So far she has no regrets—that she admits. Humor is a standard part of her every day and portrays that candidly in her increasingly popular blog. If you ask if she has children, she'll say yes, her dog Cooper.

Follow her twitter @jerricazeron
Check out her award winning blog at
www.jerricazeron.com
Like the book's Facebook Page:
Axing My Exes